Teach My Hands to War

We Wrestle Not Against Flesh

DR. D.M. RAPHAEL

Dedication

I dedicate this book to God, who is first and foremost in my life. Without You, where would I be? To my parents and grandparents: Thank you for your unwavering belief in me. To my son: Never stop believing in the goodness of God. Pursue your passions for Him with a vengeance. To my siblings: Always keep God first. Finally, to my extended family and dear friends: Thank you for encouraging me to grow into the best version of myself so that the Kingdom of God is made manifest on the earth.

Acknowledgments

I would like to take the time acknowledge Mariesa Moore-Gentry and the *Your Best Dash* brand. Thank you for helping me make this book come to life. You invested a lot of time, effort, and patience with me.

I also want to acknowledge Princess Z Lee (The Lee Group) for her assistance with helping me push the concept of the book.

I want to acknowledge Pastor Cassandra Hill for introducing me to such fabulous editors.

Disclaimer

This book is a work of fiction. All characters, names, and plots are imaginary and created by the author, Dr. D.M. Raphael (also known as Dr. Deserae Raphael or Dr. Rae). They are a culmination of various professed true accounts intertwined to create a story.

The Purpose

The purpose of this book is to give readers an understanding of what happens in the spirit realm and the natural realm from a fictional perspective. The author realizes that some people may never read the Bible, and even if they do, they might not fully understand or value it as Truth. However, by illustrating through a story how situations and plots might unfold in both the natural world and the spirit realm, the author hopes to show that life's circumstances may not be mere coincidences, luck, or chance.

This book was birthed to help people understand that they are not powerless against the Enemy, and they have authority in Christ, no matter the stage of their spiritual development. We must know how to fight against our enemies. "Blessed be the LORD my strength, which teacheth my hands to war, and my fingers to fight" (Psalm 144:1). David professed this scripture during his many battles, as noted in 1 Samuel 17:48-50 and 18:26-27. *The Enduring Word Commentary* highlights that it is dangerous to enter a battle without knowing how to use the weapons provided.

This fictional story will demonstrate ways people conduct spiritual warfare and the possible enemies they may face. Ephesians 6:12 reads: "This is not a wrestling match against a human opponent. We are wrestling with rulers, authorities, the powers who govern this world of darkness, and spiritual forces that control evil in the heavenly world" (NOG). This verse refers to the unseen powers that attempt to regulate our thoughts, desires, imagination, creativity, and relationships.

If a person believes demons exist, then it should not be far-fetched to believe angels exist. Similarly, if a person believes good exists, then it should not be hard to believe evil exists. If an individual chooses to believe Heaven is real, then it should not be hard to believe Hell is real. While some people think these forces are "make-believe" or myths, they are not. The Enemy's first trick is to convince his host that he and his cohorts do not exist so that he can freely wreak havoc on their lives.

> "And there was a war in heaven: Michael and his angels fought against the dragon; and the dragon fought against his angels, and prevailed not; neither was their place found any more in heaven. And the great dragon was cast out that old serpent, called the devil, and Satan, which deceiveth the whole world; he was cast out in the earth, and his angels were cast out with him" (Revelation 12:7-9).

Part of this story was also written about in Revelation 12:4 in the Bible. It describes how a third of the angels were cast out of Heaven with Lucifer, Satan, who was once one of God's holy angels. He no longer wanted to serve God but aspired to be equal to or become God. His pride cost him his position. He was the "Son of the Morning." Literally. He was beautiful and had pipes within him. He was dressed in precious stones, particularly onyx. But he rebelled against God and took one-third of the heavenly host (angels) with him.

> "How art thou fallen from heaven, O Lucifer, son of the morning! how art thou cut down to the ground, which didst weaken the nations! For thou hast said in thine heart, I will ascend into heaven, I will exalt my throne above the stars of God: I will sit also upon the mount of the congregation, in the sides of the north: I will ascend above the heights of the clouds; I will be like the Most High. Yet thou shalt be brought down to hell, to the sides of the pit. They that see thee shall narrowly look upon thee, and consider thee, saying, is this the man that made the earth to tremble, that did shake kingdoms; That made the world as a wilderness, and destroyed the cities thereof; that opened not the house of his prisoners? All the kings of the nations, even all of them, lie in glory, everyone in his own house. But thou art cast out of thy grave like an abominable branch, and as the raiment of those that are slain, thrust through with a sword, that go down to the stones of the pit; as a carcass trodden under feet" (Isaiah 14:12-19).

When people become saved and reject the Enemy and his kingdom, they automatically become involved in a war. Job also notes, "Man that is born of a woman is of few days and full of trouble" (Job

14:1). The Enemy hates people, whether saved or unsaved. Therefore, we must learn how to fight spiritually. Angels and demons are governed by an order with Satan's kingdom mimicking God's kingdom. Many texts, commentaries, and churches describe the order of the heavenly realm. The author will mention only a few spiritual ranks to help readers understand the parallels between God's kingdom and Satan's kingdom. Ephesians 6:12 refers to principalities, powers, rulers of darkness, and spiritual wickedness in high places in relation to Satan's kingdom. However, the Bible also mentions principalities, rulers, authorities, powers, dominions, thrones, and world rulers in various verses in relationship to both kingdoms (Colossians 1:16; Ephesians 3:10; Ephesians 1:21; Daniel 7:9).

It is the author's current understanding that each of these ranks exists in opposition to one another in the spiritual realm. When Adam and Eve sinned against God by eating from the Tree of Knowledge of Good and Evil, mankind lost its authority over the earth (Genesis 3:6; Romans 5:12; and Colossians 3:15). The Enemy had full rule over territories and kingdoms until Jesus died on the cross for our sins. He destroyed the works of the Enemy and restored mankind's authority over the earth (Colossians 3:15). Luke 10:19 states: "Behold, I give you power to tread on serpents and scorpions, and over all the power of the enemy, and nothing shall by any means hurt you."

Even though this verse refers to an isolated account of when the 70 disciples were commissioned to evangelize the cities, it is often used as a promise of God regarding spiritual warfare. Revelation 12:12 reads: "Therefore rejoice, O heaven and you who dwell in them! Woe to the inhabitants of the earth and the sea! For the devil has come down to you having great wrath, because he knows that he has a short time." Satan, the Resister, hates man. So, no matter who you are, he has an agenda to destroy you and all of mankind. But we must fight!

Nehemiah 4:14 states: "And I looked, and rose up, and said unto the nobles, and to the rulers, and to the rest of the people, be not ye afraid of them: remember the Lord, which is great and terrible, and fight for your brethren, your sons, and your daughters, your wives, and your houses." You must fight. Fight for yourselves, your family, your destiny, your legacy, and your brethren.

"Blessed be the LORD my strength, which teacheth my hands to war, and my fingers to fight" (Psalm 144:1).

Table of Contents

Chapter 1

Be on Time

At 6:00 a.m., the digital alarm clock buzzed on the end table near Paul, who lay on the edge of his bed on his stomach. He began to haphazardly slap the buzzer on the clock so hard that it fell on the floor. Paul was running late for work and was also overcoming a hangover from Sunday night. He got up and dragged himself to the bathroom, threw water on his face, and looked gruffly into the mirror. He turned on his favorite country music station. Unbeknownst to him, a demon watched him on his left side and an angel on his right. As he shaved his face, he slightly cut himself but continued with his routine.

"Ouch! I've got twenty minutes to get to work!" he exclaimed. He rushed to take a shower, put on his jeans and a T-shirt, ran down the stairs, grabbed his red and black checkered hunting jacket, boots, and hat, shook his keys, and went out the door. He rubbed his hands together for warmth as he entered the car. "Brrrr, it's cold today."

Paul drove rather fast, and people honked as he raced down the street. When he arrived at the construction site where he worked, the foreman approached the truck. "You're late," he said.

Paul solemnly replied, "I'm sorry," as he continued to drive on the rough, makeshift road of the construction site.

Tom, the office manager, greeted Paul as he entered the office to clock in. "Hey, Paul, how's it going?" Tom asked.

1

Paul grabbed his ticket, hastily punched in, and said, "I'm late. Gotta go."

Tom tried to ask him a question, but Paul ran out of the office. He went to the dump truck, and the foreman stopped him, sarcastically saying, "No, Paul, I want you on the tractor today. The dump truck is for people who can be on time."

Paul gave the foreman an insincere yet respectful, "Yes, Boss" look. When he got on the tractor, he waited for the foreman to look the other way and made a face at him, saying, "That old rust bucket."

Paul Gray is about 45 years old, stands at 6'2", and weighs 250 lbs. He has rugged weather-beaten facial features and wears his long, brown hair in a ponytail on occasion. Paul has a pug nose, rosy cheeks, and some craters on his face from bad shaving. He lives alone and works about 25 minutes from his job. His wardrobe is rustic and consists of checkered fall jackets, T-shirts, blue jeans, and black boots.

Paul grew up in Cincinnati, Ohio. His father, Jack Gray, worked as a factory worker for a dairy company. When the factory closed and Jack lost his job, he began to drink and verbally abuse Paul's mother, Elaine Gray. A kind Christian woman, Elaine loved Jack and Paul very much. She always had breakfast, lunch, and dinner ready, and she washed clothes, cooked, and cleaned. She never complained and tried to look at the best in every situation. Elaine also maintained a part-time job at Chuck's Diner in town. She lives about 35 minutes away from Paul.

Elaine loves God and goes to church every Sunday. She would drag Paul to church as a child, but she could not convince Jack to return after he lost his job. Elaine prayed for Jack's salvation until the day he died in a car accident 15 years ago. Jack had gotten drunk at a bar and decided to drive home; a truck hit him when he missed the stop sign at an intersection.

Elaine was devastated and cried every night for months. She had hoped that Jack would get another job and things would return to normal. Although she continued going to church and serving, she was never the same after Jack died. He left an insurance policy, but it was only enough to cover the funeral expenses. Now, Elaine lives off her wages from her job at the diner and social security. She doesn't always make ends meet, but she manages.

When Jack died, Paul was angry. He had watched how his father treated his mother. "How could my father do this to my mom?" Paul asked. "Why wouldn't he stop drinking? How could he do something so stupid and leave us?" Paul felt that his father did not care, and he wondered if God cared. He moved out of his parents' house a few months after the funeral. "I can't take the memories. I can't take the crying. I can't take the pain. I gotta get out of here," he said. He did not understand how God could let this happen.

Twenty-seven years ago, Paul began working at Ted's Construction Company after high school. He didn't like school much but was good with construction, lifting, and driving large trucks. He lived a simple life, working during the week and hanging out at bars with his "friends" on the weekends. He had a few lady friends here and there, but nothing serious. He liked his cramped, junky apartment and generally stayed to himself.

Mark, a longtime friend and co-worker, asked, "Hey, Paul, are you going to Tom's football party this Saturday?"

"I didn't know there was a party this Saturday. Where's it going to be?" Paul replied.

"I think at Tom's house or his church's meeting hall."

"You want me to go to church to watch a football game? Yeah, that ain't gonna work," Paul sneered.

"What do you mean?" Mark asked.

"I can just see it now. Somebody from my team makes a fumble, and then I say some 'fumbling' words. Hell busts wide open in the church, and then I'm swallowed up," Paul said.

Mark laughed hysterically.

"Besides, church ain't for sinners like me. I'll pass."

"There will be food, and I heard his wife is a great cook," Mark said.

"Naw, I don't know. I'll think about it," Paul said.

The foreman, Cal, noticed the men talking and that their 15-minute break was over. "Hey, ladies, stop cackling and get back to work."

"He sure has a way with words," Paul retorted in a high-pitched, feminine voice.

"What did you say, Paul?" Cal asked.

Mark smirked.

Paul sarcastically replied, "Coming, Boss."

Around noon, the buzzer rang for lunch. Paul went to clock out at the main office because he needed to buy a power saw from the hardware store. He saw Tom, who said, "Hey, Paul, I wanted to invite you to—"

"I know. Mark already told me. I'll think about it. I heard your wife's a good cook," Paul said.

"She sure is," Tom replied. "We'd be delighted to have you come over."

"I don't know, Preacher. Your house is too 'holy' for a guy like me."

Tom laughed. "Don't be silly. It will just be the guys—no women or children. You'll be fine," he said.

Paul reluctantly responded, "I'll let you know."

Tom Rogers is the pastor of a local church called Open Arms. He has a wife and three children: T.J., who is 8 years old, Marvin, who just turned 5, and Mary Jane, who is 2 years old. Tom has been pastoring the church for about 19 years and has been married for 15 years. He loves his family and church family. He founded the church in 2001, shortly after 9/11, feeling that God was calling him to ministry. He says the Lord commissioned him to name the church "Open Arms" because so many people are rejected by other churches for "religious reasons." He welcomes everyone, no matter what. "Go into all the world and preach the gospel to every creature" (Mark 16:15 NKJV) and "This is the Great Commission," Tom often states. He met his wife Carla soon after opening the church. She is from Puerto Rico, loves to cook, and is kind, full of life, and devoted to her family. There isn't anything she wouldn't do for Tom.

Paul got into his car and drove to the hardware store. As he walked in, he saw his mother.

"Paul… Paul… What are you doing here? Shouldn't you be at work?"

Paul turned around, surprised, and said, "Hey, Ma. I gotta pick up my saw."

Elaine checked out and walked with her items to her car. Paul noticed that she was limping, so he went over to her and said, "I got it. Why are you limping?"

"Oh, Paul, you worry too much. It's nothing."

"Have you been to the doctor?" Paul asked.

Elaine just looked at him and said, "I told you it would be alright, and no, I haven't been to the doctor yet."

Paul took her things to the car and said, "You need to get that looked at." He put her items in the car and made sure she was safely secured. "You shouldn't be driving on that leg. I love you, Ma. Call me if you need a ride to the doctor."

"I love you too, Son, and don't worry about me."

Paul didn't know that Elaine wouldn't go to the doctor because she didn't have the money.

Elaine is about 4'11," a little plump but frail in health. She is lively in spirit, full of the Spirit of God, and loves to pray. Elaine always appears cheerful in public and doesn't allow people to see her suffering. However, she does her best to help others in need. She tends to wear long skirts and short-sleeved tops. Her glasses sit at the tip of her nose because she is farsighted and has trouble seeing objects up close. When she wants to see things close up, she pulls the glasses back up to the bridge of her nose.

Paul returned to the store and picked up his saw. When he went to his car, a ticket was on the windshield. "Give me a break," Paul complained. He crumpled the ticket and threw it on the ground.

The meter attendant observed his reaction and said, "Hey, I'd treat you a lot nicer if you got here on time."

"What? Who said that?" Paul turned around and looked down at the 5'7" meter attendant, who had wavy red hair, a thin build, and was wearing a blue uniform. "I'd be a lot nicer if I didn't get this ticket."

She laughed.

"Haven't I seen you around here before?" Paul asked.

"Maybe we'll meet again if you're late," she retorted. "I'll let the ticket go this time because I saw you helping that woman."

"That woman is my mom. Thanks. I gotta go."

Paul got into his car. "Yes, I escaped another one," he said, feeling proud of himself for being able to talk his way out of things. He went back to his job and when work was finished, he clocked out and decided to go to the bar, wondering, *where do I know that lady from?*

Chapter 2
Angels vs. Demons

Paul went to a familiar bar after work and saw the bartender, Charles. "Hey Paul, what'll it be?"

"The usual," Paul replied.

"Okay, a cold brusky, no ice, coming up."

While Paul sat, one of his beer buddies came in. "You better lighten up on those beers before you fall out of that chair, Paul," Carl Santiago said. It was a real joke coming from Carl, who always drank himself into a slumber every time he came to the bar.

"Sit down and have a drink," Paul said with a laugh.

"What are you doing this weekend?" Carl asked.

"I don't know. The game is on, so I'll probably watch it at home."

"Well, I'll be here watching the game."

"You mean sleeping through it."

Carl loves to drink. He often says he is watching the game only to fall asleep after a few beers. Charles, the bartender, usually calls a taxicab or an Uber for him to go home when this happens. Carl frequents the bar to escape from his troubles at home. He is the oldest of five boys in his family. All his siblings have moved away, and he takes care of his father who has Alzheimer's disease. He fights with Carl and often asks about his deceased wife. He needs to move to an assisted living facility, but Carl doesn't have the heart to send him. Instead, a home health aide comes to care for his father during the day while Carl is at work, and a respite aide visits twice a week in the evening. Carl doesn't have many friends and comes to Charlie's Bar just to get away and escape his reality.

After a few drinks and light conversation, Paul left the bar. Nothing could have prepared him for what would happen to him while driving home. While he drove, he thought he saw a demon. *I must have had too much to drink*, he thought to himself. He safely pulled into his apartment parking lot, parked his car, entered his unit, and rested on the couch. Indeed, what he saw was a demon in the spirit realm.

Lofty, a small demon, about the size of a miniature Chihuahua, is assigned to Paul. It likes to sit on Paul's left shoulder. Paul can't see or feel it. It is dark and resembles a misshaped ghost from a Pac-Man caricature. Its job is to make sure that Paul fails, dies, or commits suicide. It hates Paul. If Lofty fails in destroying Paul, it will be sent back to hell, replaced, and tormented forever for its failure.

Paul also has an angel named Aleichem, which means "Peace be unto you." His job is to help Paul succeed, prevent him from falling into traps, guide him toward obeying the Word of God, and influence him toward his destiny. Aleichem is quite tall and wears a radiant white and gold robe. He resembles a giant man with wings and white hair.

Both the demon and the angel are unseen. They wage war against each other and try to find ways to steer or guide Paul in different directions. Paul believes in neither of them. If it weren't for Paul's mom's prayers, who knows what would have happened to him by now?

As Paul slept on the couch, he dreamed he had hit someone while driving. Restlessly tossing and turning, he woke up in a cold sweat, panting and yelling, "I drank too much! Now what?" After taking a shower, he tried to sleep again. Unfortunately, as he lay there, Lofty whispered, "Oh, just get another beer." However, Aleichem began to sing softly over Paul and sway his arms, bringing him a sense of peace that helped him drift back to sleep.

"You always interrupt," Lofty snarled.

"The Word says, 'Behold I give my beloved sleep,' Psalm 127:2."

"Well, I had plenty of worry, anxiety, and stress for him to dwell on."

"Not tonight! Leave him alone," shouted Aleichem.

Elaine's prayers have kept Paul up until this point. They have been the reason why Aleichem can comfort him in times of trouble. When Paul finally begins to develop his relationship with God, he will have to learn to use the Word of God for himself so that his angels can move on his behalf.

The next morning, Paul groggily woke up to get ready for work. He seemed to have had a good night's sleep after the initial night's ordeal, but he still couldn't get the image of hitting someone out of his head. He pictured it in his mind until he pulled up to the construction site. He clocked in and saw Tom.

"Hey, Paul."

"Hi, Tom," Paul replied with curtness.

11

"If you can't make it to the game this Saturday, maybe you can come to church on a Sunday or Wednesday."

Paul tried to be nice, but he was a little annoyed. He just did not want to go to church and wished Tom would stop inviting him to events. But he didn't have the heart to tell him directly.

"Ahh, maybe," Paul quickly replied before rushing out the door to meet Cal and get his instructions for the day.

"I want you to operate the forklift until noon and then drive the dump truck from 1:00 to 4:00 p.m.," Cal said.

As Paul walked away, Lofty whispered, "You should have told Tom to shut up, stop asking you to these stupid functions, and leave you alone."

"He is kind to you and wants to be your friend. There is no harm in that," Aleichem countered.

I just don't want to be rude, Paul thought. He heard the thoughts but didn't realize they weren't his.

Suddenly, Chief Gore summoned Lofty. An eerie whistle went off that only the demons and angels could hear. Lofty was swooped away and stood in front of Chief Gore.

"Where are you in the process?" Chief Gore demanded.

"He had a dream about hitting someone," Lofty cringed and replied.

"What is your job?" Chief Gore shouted.

"To steal, kill, and destroy," Lofty replied softly.

"So, what have you stolen, killed, or destroyed at this point?"

"Nothing," Lofty said fearfully.

"Really?" Chief Gore retorted. "You're useless, slow, and a waste of my time. What did I tell you to do?"

"Make sure he fails, dies, or commits suicide," responded Lofty.

"Did you at least plant seeds of discord?" asked Chief Gore.

"Yes," Lofty replied.

"Well, it's not enough. Get out of my sight and get the job done!"

Chief Gore is a chief demon who oversees a fleet of about 1,000 demons. They must answer to him regarding their success in destroying and tormenting people, especially saints—those who have believed in and received salvation. Chief Gore can send out as few as one or as many as thirty demons to various regions and individuals. These demons are assigned to ignite hatred, division, anger, violence, depression, confusion, racism, fear, suicide, witchcraft, unholiness, and all forms of hurt toward humans. Chief Gore is hunched-back, furry, and has cold, dark-red eyes. He wears a hideous silver crown with skulls in it and his teeth look like fangs. He wears a red cape and no shoes. If someone were to see him, they would be grossed out before they became afraid. He is just that ugly. Chief Gore must answer to an elite council of tertiary master spirits called the Thanotoshi.

This elite council makes plans for regions to promote their father, the Devil's agenda. Chief Gore is afraid of them. He must succeed at their plans or be subject to higher forms of torment in the demonic realm. Chief Gore is harsh with the lower demons because he knows it will cost him eternal torment.

The Thanotoshi has 11 members who govern all the chief spirits. Eleven is the number of chaos. Thanotoshi is a combination of the Greek and Japanese words for death. There are at least 33 chief spirits in the tri-state area who rule other legions of demons. The Thanotoshi's plans are often destroyed and halted by the children of God: the Saints. The Saints don't always realize their power or recognize that when they pray the Word of God, things get done in the spirit realm. Sometimes the solution is just invisible to them—except for those who demonstrate unwavering faith. They just pray, believe, wait, and watch the manifestation of God.

The noon lunch buzzer went off and Paul was relieved because he was ready to eat. Just as he went to lunch, he got a call on his cell phone.

"Hello?"

"Hello, may I please speak to Paul?"

"This is Paul. Who's calling?"

"This is Dr. Jones from Mt. Sinai Hospital. I hate to be the bearer of bad news, but it seems that your mother took a fall and is currently unconscious. Could you come in? We need you to fill out some paperwork as you are listed as her son and caregiver."

"I'll be right there."

After hanging up, Paul yelled, "Yo, Cal!"

"Yeah?"

"My mother is in the hospital."

"What? Sorry to hear that."

"I gotta go, and I won't be back this afternoon."

"Okay, see you later, Paul. Call when you can," said Cal.

Paul clocked out and rushed to the hospital.

Chapter 3
Accept the Invitation

Paul arrived at the hospital and rushed to the information desk. "I am here to see Elaine Gray."

"She is on the fifth floor in the Intensive Care Unit," said the receptionist.

Paul reached the fifth floor. He went to the nurse's station and asked to see Elaine Gray. Dr. Jones greeted him and said, "Your mother is in critical condition. She fell and hit her head. She also sprained her ankle and rolled on it while walking down the stairs. When she fell, one of the neighbors heard her scream. They came to the door, but she did not answer, so the neighbor called the police. The police burst the door open and found her lying on the floor, unconscious. She has not awakened yet, but her vitals are stable. There is a concern that she may have a blood clot."

"May I please see my mother?" Paul anxiously asked.

Paul rushed to see her, but nothing could prepare him for the sight of tubes in his mother's nose, her lifeless expression, and looking so alone. Tears rolled down his face as he watched her. He went to her bedside and whispered, "You have to live." He did not want to leave his mother or experience another death.

"God, please let her live. You can't do this to me again," he pleaded. "I could see someone like me... reckless, lying here, but not her.

She loves You, prays to You every night, goes to church, and believes in You no matter what. Not her. Not her. Not her."

Paul sat quietly for the next three hours. While sitting in the outward silence, the inward noise kept his mind racing. Suddenly, his cell phone rang.

"Hello?"

"How's your mother?" Cal inquired.

"She is unconscious. It seems a little bad."

"Hey, take the week off. I'll let everybody know what's going on and we'll say a prayer."

After the call ended, Paul stayed at the hospital.

Throughout the week, people from Paul's job, the church, and the neighborhood sent flowers and cards. He went home only twice to get clothes and toiletries, but faithfully stayed by his mother's side. All the while, Lofty whispered miserable words of guilt to Paul: "You should have been there. This is your fault. Why didn't you insist on taking her to the doctor? You're a sorry son. If she wakes up, she will never forgive you."

Paul tried to silence the voice. He put his hands over his ears and said, "God, forgive me. If You're real, help me." Aleichem sent a breath of peace and hope toward Paul. At that moment, he felt comforted and cried himself to sleep in the hospital chair.

On the following Saturday, Tom came to see Paul and Elaine at the hospital.

When Tom arrived, Paul was both shocked and somewhat relieved.

"Hello, Paul."

"Hey, Tom. How did you get here? There are no visitors allowed in the ICU."

"I'm a pastor. We have certain privileges."

"She still hasn't woken up," Paul said.

Very lovingly, Tom placed his hand on Paul's shoulder. "Do you need anything?"

Paul looked up and said, "Shouldn't you be at the football party?"

"It's not until later, and this is far more important."

Paul looked at Tom and then put his head down. "I need her to live. I don't have any other family."

Tom knew not to say too much to Paul at this point. The silence was golden for Paul. Tom prayed silently, gave Paul a card with some money in it, and proceeded to leave. On his way out, Paul asked, "I might take you up on your invitation to attend church this Sunday. What time is the service?"

"We start at eleven o'clock."

"I might be there."

Tom looked at Paul and said, "I hope to see you, and I am praying for you and your mother."

Paul cried again after Tom left. He just wanted his mother back. He reflected on her cooking, laughter, and singing while gardening. She used to say singing made the flowers grow. He remembered how she prayed for him, took him to church, and read the Scriptures to him. Now she was just lying there in the hospital bed.

"How is this fair?" Lofty threw a breath of despair at Paul.

Paul stared into space, and Aleichem reminded him of the Sunday School Bible stories about Jesus healing people. He remembered how Jesus had raised Lazarus from the dead, healed the blind, the deaf, and the crippled. "Would God truly do this for my mom?" Paul's faith weighed in the balance. He thought about if God would help his mother and went to sleep.

The next day, he washed up, got dressed at the hospital, and decided to go to church that morning. He was a half hour late but made it in time for the sermon. He walked in to see Tom preaching. Paul heard Tom say, "We would see Jesus. In this text, John 12:21, the Greeks have heard about how Jesus raised Lazarus from the dead. He had been dead for four days. According to Jewish tradition, you were not considered dead until after the third day. The Gentiles were looking for Jesus. How many of you would like to see Jesus?"

Something resonated with Paul. He said to himself, "That is who I am here to see. I need healing for my mom. If this Jesus is real, then He is the only one who can do it."

Lofty began to whisper in Paul's ear, "God will not listen to a wretched sinner like you. You drink, cuss... When was the last time you went to church? You're only coming for a miracle. You're a phony! God doesn't care about you!" Aleichem watched quietly, knowing that Lofty's influence was powerless in the presence of God.

Even though Lofty was in Paul's ear, Pastor Tom's preaching seemed to counteract everything Lofty said. Tom preached, "It doesn't matter who you are. He wants the wretched sinner like you. It doesn't matter if you drink, cuss, or gamble. It doesn't matter when you last attended church. The Greeks asked to see Jesus because they heard about a miracle."

This must be God. How is this man in my head? Paul said to himself.

"I am telling you today, you are the miracle! You are genuinely cared for and loved. Jesus died for you and wants to have a relationship with you. Will you come to Jesus? Will you give your life to Jesus? Will you let Him save you? Heal you?" Pastor Tom kept preaching, "Will you accept the invitation? Will you accept Christ's invitation for your life?"

A few people got up and went to the front of the church. Paul wrestled with the idea of going to the altar. He was so desperate that he did not care what Lofty said. He felt broken and empty and wanted healing for his mother. He got out of his seat and put one foot in front of the other. With each step, he felt a growing lightness, and before he knew it, he was at the front of the church. Within himself, Paul said, *I accept the invitation. I accept the invitation.*

When everyone came to the altar, Pastor Tom instructed them to repeat after him: "I am a sinner. I accept and believe that Jesus died on the cross and rose on the third day for my sins. I ask You, Jesus, to come into my life. Old things are passed away, and I am a new creature in You." With conviction, Paul and the others repeated the prayer. Paul felt renewed. He sensed a warm presence around and within him. He experienced a peace unlike anything he had felt before and knew his life would never be the same.

After church, Paul asked Tom to pray with him for his mother. Pastor Tom invited four church mothers to place their hands on Paul's shoulders as they prayed for divine healing for Elaine. "Father, please cause Elaine to wake from her coma and be healed in the name of Jesus."

Paul thanked everyone for praying for him and his mother. He felt a renewed sense of purpose and peace. He decided to check on his mother's house after church before returning to the hospital.

When Paul approached the house, he noticed the door lock was broken. *They must have left the door open when they took her to the hospital,* he thought. He quietly walked around the house and then nervously entered, thinking someone could be or had been inside. As he walked through the rooms, it appeared that no one had been there since Elaine was taken to the hospital. Nothing was missing or disturbed. "Thank God! No one has been here."

There was a pile of mail on the floor, mainly unpaid bills. *How am I going to pay these bills? I don't have access to her bank accounts.*

Paul went to the garage, grabbed a lock and some tools, and installed a temporary lock on his mother's front door before returning to the hospital.

When Paul arrived at the hospital, Dr. Jones called him over. "Paul, I need to speak with you. Your mother's vitals seem to be improving. A nurse thought she heard her speak today."

"That's good!" said Paul.

"There's a matter concerning your mother's insurance. We can't seem to find her information in the system. Does she have insurance?"

"Frankly, I don't know," Paul responded.

"Well, don't worry about it for now. We'll have a social worker handle it."

Paul walked into his mother's room. He sat down and thought about all the things that happened. He began to talk to his mother. "Mom, you would have been proud of me today. I gave my life to the Lord. Yeah, that's right. I went to church."

"Oh... uh... it's about time," his mother said weakly.

Paul looked up at her, tears in his eyes. "Mom, you're awake! You're awake!"

"I've been asking for water, but no one could hear me."

Paul rushed to the nurse's station. "She's awake! She's awake! She asked for water."

The nurses hurried to Elaine's room, but she was out again.

"Ma, Ma!"

Her eyes opened again. The head nurse said, "Go get the doctor."

Chapter 4
Mom's Surgery

Dr. Jones examined Elaine and asked Paul to step outside. He waited in the hallway. When Dr. Jones came out, she said, "Upon examining your mother, it seems she is recovering. An angiography taken a few days ago revealed that she has a blood clot in her leg. We don't want it to travel to her heart or brain. Since she is more cognizant now, I want to start her on blood thinners. She might be in and out of consciousness for the next few days, but it seems as if she will come around."

Paul let out a partial sigh of relief and said to himself, *God, You are real. I don't deserve this. Thank You!*

The next day, Paul went back to work. "Hey, Tom. I can't thank you enough for praying for me and my mom. She's awake."

"That is great news. Praise the Lord!" Tom shouted. "If you need anything, let me know."

Paul went outside to receive his orders for the day.

"You're on the truck for today," Cal said. "Take it easy."

Paul kept thinking about his mother. After work, he went to the hospital. When he arrived, Dr. Jones greeted him.

"Hello, Paul. Your mom seems to be a little better. A social worker arrived today to help with the billing and insurance. I am a bit concerned about the blood clot and how she keeps going in and out. We used an ultrasound to find the first blood clot, but a second test with an MRI revealed that there are more than one. We will need to perform a thrombectomy to remove the additional blood clots."

Paul felt a bit overwhelmed by the news. "When do you plan to do the surgery?" he asked.

"Tomorrow," Dr. Jones replied. "I am concerned that waiting too long could lead to a stroke, given the location of the clot. I'm going to stop the blood thinners for now," Dr. Jones explained.

While Paul and the doctor conversed, Elaine had horrible dreams. An angel and a demon were assigned to her. The demon continually harassed her as she slept. She dreamed that something was chasing her. Typically, Elaine's prayer life was strong. If something was bothering her, she would pray to God or read her Bible, and she would get through it. Unfortunately, she couldn't follow her usual routine of praying and reading her Bible due to her condition. A spirit of fear began to influence her mind because of the fall. This demon was named Sane, pronounced "Saw-nay," which is the Hebrew word for hate. He hates, hates, hates Elaine. She prayed a lot, and he almost always lost with his plans to destroy her.

Repetitively, Elaine kept dreaming that she was being chased. Each time she reached the end of the stairs, the demon would push her down. Her angel needed some activation. Angels move at the Word of God through our prayers.

Paul walked into the room and watched his mother as she lay asleep. Every so often, she would cry out, "No. Don't push me," and

Paul would begin to pray. Paul gingerly spoke. "God, you know my mother. Jesus, You healed the blind and the deaf and brought a man back to life. I ask You to heal my mother and bring her peace while she sleeps."

At that moment, Elaine's angel began to play the violin, causing a peaceful sleep to overtake her. Elaine's angel is named Shamar, which means "to guard." He is very protective of her and does all he can to help. However, if she is stubborn or resistant to the Holy Spirit's leading, Shamar cannot do much. This concept of protection resonates with all angels. The Holy Spirit had urged Elaine to go to the doctor, but she had refused. Shamar can only do so much or as directed based on the Word of God. She must do her part and be obedient to His Word—whether spoken or written, as stated in Psalm 91:11: "For He shall give His angels charge over thee to keep thee in all thy ways."

After Paul prayed, some unseen conversations transpired between his and Elaine's angels and demons.

"What are you looking at?" Lofty asked Aleichem.

"Nothing," retorted Aleichem.

"You know I am going to make sure Paul dies."

"No weapon formed against him shall prosper," Aleichem stated.

"I don't need to worry about my person dying. There she is and it's just a matter of days. My assignment will be done, promotion in place, and on to the next victim," Sane said to Lofty.

"Surely, you jest," said Shamar. "After 35 years of trying, you still haven't learned."

"Healing is the children's bread," said Shamar. "She will not die but live to declare the works of the Lord. You have no power."

"I don't need it," Sane retorted. "I have sickness, despair, and doubt to back me up this time."

"Well, there goes your promotion," Shamar said.

"What do you mean?" asked Sane.

"Hmm, let's think. You need three more demons to help you. And let's see—it has taken you over 35 years to do the obvious. Look forward to your demotion. She will live."

"Hey, Sane," said Lofty. "How about you and I make some plans for their demise?"

"Hmm...I'm not sure," Sane said.

"It will be a win-win," Lofty said.

"When was the last time you won?" Sane asked.

Aleichem and Shamar just stared at each other with confident looks. They are confident that God will prevail.

Paul called his job to tell them he wouldn't be in the next day due to his mother's surgery. Then he went to sleep in the hospital chair. Meanwhile, Tom felt led to start a prayer chain for Elaine and contacted some of the church's prayer warriors to pray for her.

The next morning, Dr. Jones entered the room and gently woke Paul. "Your mother will be prepped for surgery at 9:00. She will go into surgery around 9:45, and it should be finished by 11:00."

"Is she going to be okay?" Paul asked.

"I think she will be fine. It's a routine procedure."

Elaine was prepped for surgery, and the anesthesiologist administered a moderate dose of anesthesia. Shamar spoke peace to Elaine as she slept, and the surgeon began to operate.

Meanwhile, Sane slowly crept in and started with the recurring dream again. As a result, Elaine started running again toward the cliff this time. The entity pushed her, and when Elaine fell in the dream, she started to lose her breath.

The nurse said, "Her heartbeat is erratic; she seems to be going into cardiac arrest. Get the electric paddles! We're losing her!"

The nurse grabbed the paddles. "One, two, three, clear!" Shamar went to Elaine in her dream. He bought her to the edge of the cliff again. He spoke to her and said, "You know the Word." The demon appeared again in the dream, but this time, she did not feel nervous.

The nurse said, "There is a heartbeat! She is stabilizing."

Elaine looked straight at the demon and said, "I won't be afraid of the terror by night nor the arrow that flieth by day. He shall give His angels charge over me to keep me in all my ways."

The demon, Sane, backed up.

"Leave!" Elaine said.

He hissed at her and made an awful face to scare her, but to no avail.

"No weapon formed against me shall prosper," Elaine said.

"Enough!" Shamar said to Sane.

Sane reluctantly and furiously left because he could not scare Elaine to death.

The surgeon completed the surgery. The nurse cleaned Elaine and took her to the ICU. As Paul prayed and paced back and forth in the hallway, Dr. Jones approached him and explained that Elaine was recovering in the ICU.

"Elaine went into cardiac arrest during the surgery, but we revived her. We were able to get the blood clots removed." Paul let out a deep sigh of relief. "You can go up to the ICU room in about 15 minutes." He was thankful that his mother was alive.

Chapter 5

My Church Family

In the coming days, Elaine slowly recovered in the hospital. Paul started attending Open Arms Church regularly, and he especially enjoyed Bible Study. One day at Bible Study, he noticed a familiar face: the meter attendant who had given him a ticket. After Bible Study, he approached her and said, "I didn't know you attended this church."

"Be careful, Buddy. I still owe you a ticket," she said, looking at him.

Paul laughed. "What's your name?"

"Reese," she replied. "I saw you the day you gave your life to the Lord."

"How come you didn't say anything?" Paul asked.

"I felt bad, and I knew you were going through something. How is your mother?" Reese asked.

"She is recovering and finally went home this past Monday. She has been in rehab for about two months," Paul said.

"That's great!" said Reese. "Maybe I will see you next Wednesday."

"You will," Paul replied with a partial smile.

Elaine went home and required a nurse during the day, along with physical therapy twice a week for three months. A social worker took care of the medical expenses from the hospital, but Elaine had a lot of bills and her mortgage to catch up on since her hospital stay. She did not want to tell Paul, but he knew she was behind.

Paul stopped by the house on Thursday after work to fix the door more permanently. When he arrived, the nurse was leaving. He went up to his mother's room and asked, "How are you doing today, Ma?"

Elaine just looked at Paul and wept. She was weak, emotional, and had lost her pride. Paul went over to her and asked, "What's the matter?"

"Paul, I didn't want to tell you, but I'm behind on the mortgage. I have enough to pay the house bills, but I'm two months behind on the mortgage, and I'm afraid they're going to foreclose on the house." She buried her face in her hands and cried some more.

"Ma, don't worry. God can handle it. I'll pick up some extra hours and call the mortgage company tomorrow. Don't worry about it. Get some rest. I'm going to fix the front door and then head home."

Paul hated to see his mother cry. *She is such a strong woman, but right now, she needs someone to be strong for her. God, the truth is I honestly don't know how to handle this. I just caught up on my house bills after taking so much time off to care for Mom at the hospital,* he thought to himself. Paul fixed the door and left. He decided to ask Pastor Tom and Cal for extra hours when he got to work on Friday.

Paul arrived at work about 15 minutes early the next day. When he saw Tom he said, "Hey, do you think I could pick up some more overtime? I'm trying to help my mom with some of her bills."

"I will look into it, Paul. We are running a little slow on overtime hours this month, but I'll do my best."

"Thanks."

Paul proceeded to work his shift. At lunch, he decided to go into town to eat. While there, he ran into Carl, his old bar buddy.

"Hey, Paul! How have you been?" Carl asked. "I heard about your mother. Is she okay?"

"She's fine," Paul responded. "Recovery is taking a bit longer than I wanted it to be, but I'm just happy she's alive. I've been attending Open Arms Church for a couple of Sundays. You should come."

"What can God do for me?" Carl replied. "All my brothers have left; my mom is dead; my father has Alzheimer's disease, and, not to mention, I'm unmarried and overweight. Why did all this happen to me?"

Paul gently took a step back. He looked at Carl and said, "I get it. I understand. When my father died, I felt the same way. You know, I had many questions: 'Why did my father drink so much?' 'Why did he die?' 'God, why did this happen?' 'God, are You there? Do You care?' When my mom got sick, I began to go to church. I realized the obvious: God was always there, but I wasn't letting Him in. He had answers, mercy, forgiveness, and love, but I wouldn't accept them. I always wanted answers, and I wanted them my way. I wouldn't pray, just complain. I wouldn't wait, seek, or listen to God. So, I got exactly what I put out—

negativity, unhappiness, and no answers. When I humbled myself, God began to give me peace and answers. The answers weren't always what I wanted or when I wanted them, but I knew it was God. Carl, if I can't get you to go to church, do you think you could at least try Jesus?"

"Uh, I don't know," Carl said with a puzzled look on his face. "Again, what can God do for me?"

"Number one," began Paul, "He can save your soul from Hell. Number two, He'll help you with guidance and direction for your life. Number three, He can give you peace. I just don't want you to leave this earth without knowing Him."

"What, are you some kind of Jesus freak now?" Carl asked sarcastically. "Paul, thanks for the invite, but I'm okay for now. I'll think about it." Uncomfortable, Carl scurried away and thought to himself, *who does he think he is now? I liked the old Paul. I feel like I'm losing a friend.*

Paul was disappointed that he couldn't sway Carl to come to church or accept Jesus. He said to God, "Please don't let him leave this earth without knowing You."

Paul proceeded to get his lunch from the deli and ate it in his car. He had pastrami on rye, a side of coleslaw, and a soda. While he ate, he saw Reese, the meter attendant, walking down the street. Paul yelled from his car, "Aren't you done giving out those unwanted presents?"

"Who said that?" Reese asked, looking around. Suddenly, her eyes found and were fixed on Paul. "Oh, it's you! Do you ever go to work?"

Paul laughed.

"How's your mother?"

"She's getting better by the day. Thanks for asking."

Moments felt like hours, and finally, with a racing heartbeat, Paul asked, "Hey, would you like to go out sometime?"

"You're asking me out?"

"Yeah," said Paul with underlying nervousness.

"It's about time!" Reese retorted. "I thought you'd never ask."

Paul liked Reese. She was fun, easy on the eyes, and had a witty personality. He liked the fact that they went to the same church.

"I will call you."

"I doubt it. You don't have my number," Reese said.

Paul laughed again. "What's your cell phone number?"

"555-241-5870," Reese replied.

After saying their farewells, Paul went back to work with a smile on his face. When he arrived, Tom said, "I can give you one extra shift this week."

"Thank you very much. Every little bit helps," Paul said.

Tom was very disappointed. "I wish I could do more."

Tom's demon's name was Enochos, which means "in danger of or guilty of." He constantly spoke to him: "You ain't no pastor. Everyone knows what your father did and where you come from. You're going to get found out, Tom."

When this happens Tom retorts, "I am the righteousness of God; I am the righteousness of God. No weapon formed against me shall prosper."

Tom's secret was that his father was the one who had accidentally killed Paul's father. Tom's name was different from his father's because of a divorce. Many years ago, Tom's mother changed his last name to her maiden name to avoid public shame. When Tom was growing up, he lived a few towns over with his mother. It ate him alive every time he saw Paul. He felt like a hypocrite and wanted to tell Paul the truth.

I know. I will raise a church donation to help Paul with his mother's bills, Tom sat and thought. He made a few phone calls to raise money for Paul but still felt guilty and unprepared to face him.

Tom also had an angel named Etan. Etan means "strength" and he was indeed strong. He could fight 30 demons alone and win. Tom needed an angel like Etan because of the immense stress he faced in the ministry, family, and job. Etan did not talk much; he just did what had to be done. One time, when Enochos kept torturing Tom in his sleep, Etan let out an ear-crushing roar that caused Enochos to scream and flee. Of course, no humans could hear the sound, but at least Tom benefited from it.

When Sunday morning arrived, Paul got up, showered, shaved, and got dressed. He sang his favorite church song, albeit out of key: "I get joy when I think about what He's done for me. I get joy when I think about what He's done for me. I come to clap my hands."

Elaine could not go to church, so she watched from her computer. Paul set it up so that she could view it virtually. Paul walked into church and listened to the sermon. As he listened, he reminisced about how his life had changed since he started attending Open Arms. He enjoyed the Word, the people, and he was also really starting to like Reese. She would wave to him during church.

As Pastor Tom was finishing up the sermon, he proclaimed, "We wrestle not against flesh and blood but principalities, powers, rulers of darkness, spiritual wickedness in high places. Psalm 144:1 also states, 'Blessed be the LORD my strength, who teacheth my hands to war and my fingers to fight.' You must fight to do God's will in your life!"

Once finished, he said, "Church, I have an announcement. Paul, could you please come to the front of the church?" Paul felt roughly embarrassed, and his face turned red. He walked to the front. One of the older church mothers walked over to him. Tom said, "We wanted to help you and your mother during this time. You have been faithful; we are truly glad to have you and wanted to say that we are here for you."

The mother of the church, Mom Susan, walked over and gave Paul an envelope. He said, "Thank you," and sat in his seat. The church clapped. When he sat down, he opened the envelope and found $3,500 inside. It was enough to cover Elaine's mortgage and then some. Paul sat in his seat in shock and full of gratitude. *Time and time again, God, You keep showing me who You are. Thank You, and thank You for my church family,* he thought to himself.

Chapter 6
The Slip, The Fall, The Hit

When Paul arrived at Elaine's house that Sunday, she was upstairs rejoicing. She had watched the live stream and could not believe what had happened. She said she would do something special for the pastor and his wife once she got better. Paul quickly paid all her bills the next day. With each bill settled, he felt more and more relief.

Elaine kept getting therapy and feeling better. She was using a walker and could bathe herself. Paul and Reese started dating. He would pick her up and take her to lunch or the movies. One day, while out with Reese, he saw Carl standing at the bus stop.

"Hey, I don't see you at the bar much now that you've been going to church. You too good for us bar folks now?" Carl asked.

"Hey, Carl! This is Reese."

"Oh, now I get why you ain't been comin' around."

"Hello," Reese said.

"Hello," Carl replied in a deep phony voice.

Paul laughed. He knew Carl did not talk like that.

"I will leave you guys to it." As he was getting on the bus, Carl said, "Why don't you come down this Thursday to watch the game?"

"I'll think about it," Paul replied.

Once Carl was completely on the bus, Reese asked, "Are you really going to go to a bar after all this time?"

"Awe, it's just one harmless beer and a football game. What could possibly happen?"

"Oh, you know evil companions corrupt good manners," Reese retorted.

"There is nothing evil about Carl, a beer, and a football game."

"I get it but be careful." Reese admonished. "I don't know why I have such a bad feeling about this. I hope it's just nerves."

"You worry too much." Paul scuffed.

Paul went to Bible Study that Wednesday, where Tom spoke on temptation. Paul took notes but did not think about how the message may have applied to his current situation with Carl. Lofty began plotting. "First, I am going to make sure that Paul gets stone drunk. I've been sending messages to Carl to be a little jealous, and it's working. Next, I am going to convince Paul, in his drunken stupor, to drive home. Then he will repeat the same mistake his father made, and my job will be done."

"Silence!" Aleichem commanded. "You will not kill him, and he will not kill himself. I have strict orders from the Lord that he is to live and not die. He has a purpose and a destiny."

"We'll see about that—won't we?" Lofty said slyly.

Paul went to Charlie's Bar for the game that Thursday. He walked in like it was home but felt a little uneasy because he had stopped drinking.

"What will it be, Paul?" Charlie asked.

"I'll take a soda."

Carl laughed. "Aww, come on, Paul. You haven't gone soft on me, have you?"

"I don't need to be drinking. I need to stay sober for my mom."

"Leave him alone. He hasn't been in the bar for 10 minutes, and you're already trying to get him drunk. He'll drink when he's ready," Charlie said.

"Give him a round of his usual on me when he's ready," Carl said.

Paul watched the game and roared when his team scored. Later on, he saw the drink Carl had bought him. He was thirsty and had finished his soda, so he drank his usual, thinking it wouldn't hurt to have one. But when he finished, he wanted another.

Carl said, "There goes the Paul I know."

Paul had yielded to temptation. He had another and another beer. Now he was slightly drunk and wanted to go home. He took his keys and started toward the door.

With an "I'm fine," Paul went to his car. Lofty

started laughing. "My plan is working."

Paul got into the car and said, "God, I'm sorry. If you have any mercy for me, please let me get home safely." He drove slowly and got home safely. He went upstairs to his apartment and fell asleep on the couch.

When Paul woke up the next morning, he had a headache and realized he was running late. He ran to take a shower when, suddenly, he had to sit down. He had drunk too much and had a hangover. He eventually took a shower and got dressed. He put on his jeans, shirt, and jacket before running out the door. Paul put the key in the ignition and sped off.

"Just call the job and let them know you will be late. Stop speeding," Aleichem whispered.

Paul arrived at the rock construction site and continued speeding toward the parking area. As he headed to the parking area, he put on his brakes. He saw a little kid in the parking lot. At first, he thought his eyes were deceiving him, but it was too late; he hit the little boy. The boy's little body flew into the air like a lifeless feather and hit the ground hard. A woman nearby screamed. It was Carla, the pastor's wife. The little boy was Marvin, their second son. A look of petrified horror overtook Paul. Then the nightmare he had a few weeks ago returned to him. Tom came out to see what the commotion was only to find his son lying on the ground with blood streaming from his head.

"Call 9-1-1!" Cal yelled.

Mark ran to get the cell phone, while Paul sat in the car in shock. His face was pale white.

Tom cried out to God, "Save my son!"

Carla cried and prayed in Spanish. Her other two children sat in the car, watching and crying. Moments later, police and ambulance sirens wailed in the distance and grew louder until they arrived. The EMTs jumped out, quickly assessed the situation, and whisked Marvin into the ambulance. Tom hastily jumped in with him. Carla frantically drove behind the ambulance and continued to pray through her sobs.

The police walked around to gather witness statements. There were several bystanders and helping hands present. Everyone recounted what they saw and heard. When the police approached Paul, he just sat there and said in a plea of desperation, "I hit the boy, but I did not mean it."

The officer asked Paul if he had consumed any alcohol or drugs, to which Paul confessed that he had been drinking the night before. The police informed Paul that he had to come down to the precinct for further questioning. Paul lowered his head in shame as he rode in the back of the police car.

When Paul arrived at the station, the officer administered a breathalyzer test, which confirmed that Paul had alcohol in his system. The officer said, "We're going to have to arrest you for driving under the influence."

"I thought I slept it off," Paul replied.

"I'm not sure, but you seem slightly hungover," said the officer.

Paul cried out, "Oh, no! Is he dead?"

Paul was offered one phone call to a lawyer, but he refused at the time. He thought about how he could not face his mother. Reese was right. The only other person he would have called was Tom, whom he had just hurt. Paul cried, "God, help me!" But he heard and felt nothing other than silence.

Lofty said to Aleichem, "Now, you see my plan is working. My plan was not to kill Paul last night. It was to have him kill himself because of the guilt. Now, I will spend time replaying his father's death and this situation over and over in his head. My work is done whether Marvin lives or dies."

Aleichem went to comfort Paul with peace.

Paul cried most of the night as he sat in his cell. He wondered if Marvin was dead or alive and asked himself if Tom and Carla hated him. The cell was cold, and the blanket given to him was a harsh wool-like material. As he lay there, he replayed Marvin's body flying through the air and the blood pouring from his head. He cried again and again. Aleichem came with peace, but Paul was too unsettled to receive it. When he fell asleep, Aleichem would try to comfort him, but it was during those times that Lofty would bring up dreams about his father or Marvin. Paul was tormented and could not remember a scripture or a prayer.

The next day, a cold silence engulfed Paul as he lay in the jail bed. The officer told Paul to get ready for his arraignment, so he washed and dressed in the jail clothes provided. A swarm of reporters attacked Paul with questions and camera flashes as he was taken for his arraignment. He held his head down.

"Paul, what caused you to drink?"

"Isn't Tom Rogers your pastor?"

"Is it true that the church just gave you a donation for your mother?"

"What was your motive?"

Then one reporter said something that Paul would never forget. "Did you attempt to kill the pastor's son because the pastor's father killed your father?"

Paul, stunned at the question said, "You animals. I would never attempt to kill a child. Why would you say that?"

But the reporters were relentless. "Isn't it true that the pastor's father killed your father about 15 years ago?"

Paul, stunned again by the questioning, became quiet and got into the car. *What was that reporter talking about? Is it true?*

Paul wondered how Marvin was doing. "Why won't anyone tell me anything? God help me!" he screamed while he sat in the police car.

Chapter 7

The Arraignment

Paul anxiously waited in another cell until his court-appointed lawyer arrived. While waiting, he tried to push the reporter's question out of his mind. But Lofty began taunting him: "You're a failure. What if you killed that little boy? Doesn't that make you a murderer, a drunk, and a loser? You're so much like your father. Your mother will never forgive you. You should just die." On and on, Lofty berated Paul.

Paul slowly looked into the jail mirror. Tears welled in his eyes as he called out to God. "Please, forgive me. Please deliver me." The transportation officer remained silent as Paul cried.

Aleichem reminded Paul of a scripture: "When the wicked, even mine enemies and my foes, came upon me to eat up my flesh, they stumbled and fell. Though a host should encamp against me, my heart shall not fear: though war should rise against me, in this will I be confident" (Psalm 27:2). A wave of peace surrounded Paul. He was brought out of the cell in handcuffs and escorted to a room. The reporters again shouted questions and took pictures as he walked down the hall to meet his lawyer.

"Hello, Mr. Gray. My name is Attorney Levi Halakah. People call me Attorney Lee for short. I've reviewed your case, and I see that you had some alcohol the night before the accident. Is that correct?"

"Yes," Paul replied.

"What happened?"

"I went out for drinks and to watch the game the night before. I went home drunk, went to sleep, and woke up late for work. I showered and got dressed, then left for work in a hurry. When I arrived at the parking lot of the site, I went to the park, the little boy ran out in front of the car, and I hit him. He flew into the air and landed on his head."

"How much did you drink?"

"I don't know. At least two or three beers."

"If the boy lives, you're looking at two to five years in prison. With good behavior maybe three years. If he dies, you are looking at five to fifteen years."

"Prison?! I can't go to prison. My mom needs me."

"Hey, I get it," Attorney Levi replied. "But right now, you have a little boy in the hospital who's in critical condition. He has significant head trauma and there's a question about whether he will be able to walk if he should come out of this coma."

Paul looked at the ground. He felt so guilty.

"There is also this question about motive," Attorney Levi stated. "Did you know that Pastor Tom's father was the man responsible for killing your father?"

Paul was stifled and bewildered by the attorney's question. He screamed and stood up. "What do you mean? What do you mean?"

The bailiff came into the room because of the commotion Paul caused. "Sit down or you will be detained. Sit down! Sit down!" The bailiff yelled.

Attorney Levi stared at Paul. "You didn't know?"

Paul broke down and cried. He *truly* didn't know. Questions flooded his heart, and he thought he would drown. With a knot in his throat, he uttered the question, "What will happen if the boy dies?"

"Again, you're looking at five to fifteen years," Attorney Levi said.

Is that why he was always so nice to me? Is God punishing me? Is Mom okay? What will she think of me? Will she be okay? Reese was right. I shouldn't have gone to the bar that night. Now look! I can barely hold it together. The church probably hates me. I will never be able to live this down, Paul thought to himself.

The bailiff came back to the room. "The judge will see you now."

Attorney Levi and Paul walked into the courtroom. Paul saw many people from church and his mother. He could tell that she had been crying. He also saw Reese; she was upset, too.

"All rise for the Honorable Judge Gracen," the bailiff said.

Judge Gracen was an older man with all-white hair. He was a no-nonsense judge who did not tolerate drunk drivers.

"You may be seated."

The bailiff handed Judge Gracen the file.

"Your Honor, this is the case of the State vs. Paul Gray. Mr. Gray is accused of hitting Marvin Rogers, a five-year-old boy, while under the influence."

"How do you plead?"

"Your Honor, we plead not guilty."

Paul was stunned by Attorney Levi's response. He looked over and whispered, "What are you doing?"

The crowd erupted into quiet chatter. Judge Gracen struck the gavel and said, "That's enough. That is enough. Order in the court!"

"You stated that the boy ran in front of your car. He was unsupervised when you hit him," Attorney Levi whispered to Paul. "Those are grounds for negligence on the part of the parents, which could reduce your sentence."

"Don't do that," Paul whispered back. "The parents are going through enough."

"Listen, Paul, that's how the game is played. You are probably going to jail but not for as long as they want you to," Attorney Levi said.

The State was represented by Attorney Jim Kategoros, a tall, thin man who wore glasses. Mr. Kategoros was always classically dressed in a light gray-silver suit. He changed his ties but kept to his silver suits. It was said that whenever he thought he was going to win, he would wear a black suit and a red tie. He was very peculiar and had a way of getting people to overreact. He walked slyly and he made dramatic pauses in the middle of his arguments.

"Are you representing the State?" Judge Gracen asked Mr. Kategoros.

"Yes, Your Honor," Mr. Kategoros replied.

"Please state your case."

"Your Honor, the State plans to prove that Mr. Gray is guilty of endangering the welfare of a minor and/or vehicular homicide if this child dies, drunk driving, and revenge."

Paul put his head down as he listened to Mr. Kategoros' words.

"We are asking for fifteen years to life in jail, no parole, and that Mr. Paul Gray be denied bail."

"Attorney Levi, what do you have to say?"

"We plead not guilty." A soft murmur filled the courtroom. "We aim to prove that it was Mr. and Mrs. Rogers' negligence that caused the incident. My client was not drunk at the time of the accident." The crowd began chattering again. "The boy in question was left unattended by his parents at the time of the incident. We also plan to prove that my client was not acting maliciously, and this was a tragic accident. While my client's alcohol level was elevated, he was not legally drunk. We are seeking the minimum amount of jail time and ten thousand dollars bail."

Paul mumbled under his breath, "What are you doing? I am guilty and I hit the little boy. Stop this! You are making me look worse!"

Paul stood up and shouted, "I'm guilty! I'm guilty! Stop this!"

Judge Gracen shouted, "There will be order in my court! Attorney Levi, get your client under control!"

"Your Honor, may I have a brief recess and a word with my client in private?"

"You may," Judge Gracen replied. "We will take a twenty-minute recess and reconvene."

Once the pair was behind closed doors, Attorney Levi shouted, "What are you doing? You have a good chance of getting no sentence or a reduced sentence, and you're throwing it all away! Why?"

"I am guilty!" Paul screamed back. "Can't you see that? And blaming the parents for my mistake is just wrong. I would never intentionally hit somebody, let alone a child." Paul sobbed. "I definitely don't want to blame my pastor, his wife, or the child for my mistake."

"Listen, Paul. I see where you're coming from, but that is not how the law works."

"Oh, God!" Paul sobbed again.

"Didn't you say you have a mother to take care of?" asked Attorney Levi. "How are you going to support her from jail?"

"I don't know. Is there a way to get the State to drop the charges?" Paul asked.

"No, you are either guilty with time or acquitted. The only way to get an acquittal is to establish reasonable doubt. The only way to demonstrate reasonable doubt is to prove the other party's negligence and establish your sobriety. There is no getting around this. Let me do my job."

Paul pondered everything that was happening. If he got out, would he even have a job? How would he take care of his mother then? He would have to move and send her money or pay her bills virtually, somehow. Either way, life as he knew it was never going to be the same. He kept thinking about his mother and how she needed care.

"Okay. Do what you have to do."

Paul and Attorney Levi walked back into the courtroom.

"All rise," the bailiff said.

The court stood at attention as Judge Gracen re-entered the room.

"Be seated," the bailiff said,

Judge Gracen proceeded to speak. "In light of the evidence presented we will have a trial. Bail will not be granted at this time. If this child should die, you could be a flight risk."

Paul thought about his mother and the suffering of Tom's son. He hung his head as the crowd murmured again. Ms. Elaine let out a cry.

The trial was set for six weeks.

Paul was escorted back to a jail cell with Attorney Levi walking alongside him. "I will be speaking with you shortly," Levi said.

Meanwhile, Reese held onto Elaine as she cried.

Paul met with Attorney Levi after the arraignment. "Listen, Judge Gracen is notorious for being hard on drunk drivers. My job is to create enough reasonable doubt to get your accuser's request rejected."

"I understand. Listen, I just want to talk to my mother to see if she is okay. Is it possible for her to communicate with me?"

"What is her number?" Levi asked.

"555-702-2117."

"I'll contact her as soon as I leave. I'll also be reviewing your alcohol level report. Who was with you the night before the incident?"

"I was at Charlie's Bar with my friend Carl, watching the game."

"What's his number?"

"I don't remember. Do you think you could tell me how Marvin is doing?" Paul asked.

"No information has been released yet, just that he is in critical condition."

Paul was escorted to another jail cell and went to lie down. As he tried to sleep, Lofty searched for another opportunity to destroy him. "I am going to pose as his father in his sleep and condemn him. He will never rest."

Aleichem overheard Lofty's plan and thought to himself, perhaps I can counteract this disaster.

While Paul slept, Lofty showed him fuzzy visions of his father. The voice that seemed like his father called him and Paul called back to it.

"Paul!   Paul!"

"Dad, is that you?"

The voice continued to call and drift. When Paul got closer to what he thought was his father, Lofty's wretched spirit appeared. He laughed at Paul and taunted, "You're guilty. You're guilty. You're guilty."

Paul woke up panting for air. How he wished he could take this situation back. How he wished he had listened to Reese.

Aleichem whispered to Paul, "No weapon formed against you shall prosper."

This thought comforted Paul; however, the guilt was beginning to get to him. Aleichem blew a trumpet, which brought calmness to Paul and caused Lofty to go away. Aleichem knew that Paul's state of mind was a matter of life and death.

Chapter 8
Marvin

Marvin lay in the hospital bed, hooked up to multiple tubes. His mother, by his side, cried, "I just turned my head for a second to give Tom the tickets. If he dies, this is my fault. I shouldn't have left him in the car alone with his siblings. How will Tom ever forgive me? He told me to stop leaving the kids in the car for those 'quick seconds.' All I had to do was call Tom from my cell phone and he would have come to the car and gotten the tickets. Now, look!"

Marvin was in his dream state, a coma. His angel, Simcha, took him to Heaven, and he played with the other kids who had been taken from Earth earlier. While Marvin was in a coma, he was kept alive with machines. Marvin's eternal spirit and soul were alive. He did not understand what was going on when he saw his body lying on the hospital bed. His soul was lifted into the air and staring at what was happening in the hospital room. He was only five years old and had no experience with death. He asked Simcha, "Why is Mommy crying?"

"She misses you, but she will see you again."

"What is your name?" Marvin asked.

"Simcha. Let's go play!"

Simcha took Marvin to Heaven.

Dr. Good entered the room. "Hello, Mrs. Rogers. Your son is in stable condition. He has sustained a massive head injury and there is significant swelling. We need to do a craniotomy to prevent the brain from continuing to swell against his skull. He also has swelling around his spine and we're not sure that he will be able to walk."

"Oh, God!" Carla sighed.

Tom walked in right as she sighed. He had just arrived after picking up the kids from school and taking them to their grandmother's house. "What is the matter?"

"They have to do a craniotomy, and they said there is swelling around his spine. They're not sure if he will walk again."

Tom hugged Carla and said, "We must walk in faith, so do not say another word. Do not give place to the Devil or this report. Dr. Good, do what you need to do, and Carla and I will be praying. He was wounded for our transgressions, bruised for our iniquities; the chastisement of our peace was upon Him, and by His stripes Marvin is healed," proclaimed Pastor Tom.

Marvin had the emergency surgery. It seemed to go well, but the swelling on his spine hadn't subsided. Carla asked Tom how court went, but Tom did not want to tell her. He simply said there was going to be a hearing in six weeks. If Carla knew what Attorney Levi had said about their negligence concerning the situation, it would crush her. Tom understood that Paul's lawyer was trying to defend him. He knew Paul felt awful and wanted to run to him when he had his outburst in court. He still felt guilty about knowing that his father had killed Paul's father.

The weight of the whole situation seemed to fall heavily on his shoulders. Tom decided to stay at the hospital with Marvin to give Carla a break and to pick up the kids.

A few mothers from the church came to the hospital looking for Pastor Tom. They were not allowed in the ICU where he was, so he came out to meet them and asked, "What are you doing here?"

"Oh, Tom, we came to support you and the family," said Joan.

Sandy gave him an envelope with some money in it and said, "We took a collection."

Tom looked at them lovingly and said, "Please pray for Marvin's healing. Have you gone to see Elaine, Paul's mother, or Paul?"

The mothers stood silently. "Uh, uh, oh—not yet," said Sister Karen.

"Please take this money and give it to her instead. Please go minister to her. I know she is sad and lonely. Do not turn your back on Elaine or Paul during this difficult time. Show the love of God to them. Be the hands and feet for me while I attend to my son. Will you do this for me, please?"

The mothers stood in shock and shame. They thought they were doing the will of the Father by supporting their pastor. However, he was showing them that he still had the undying love of God and mercy for someone who had wronged him and his family.

Mother Sandy said to the other mothers, "We need to practice what we've been taught. Love God and others. Not just the ones we self-righteously believe deserve our kindness."

The mothers did as they were asked and went to see Elaine. They arrived and rang the doorbell. Elaine hobbled slowly to the door with her cane because her ankle was still healing. She opened the door and saw the church mothers. One of them said, "We are here to support you at this time. Can we come in?"

"Come on in," Elaine replied.

Her house was in slight disarray because she had left abruptly with Reese when she found out what had happened.

"How are you?" Mother Joan asked.

Elaine burst out in tears and Joan embraced her.

Mother Sandy went to the store to ensure Elaine had enough food in the refrigerator for a few days while the other mothers cleaned the house. Some of them gave Elaine money to pay a few bills. They helped her to her room so she could rest. Reese would come by throughout the week to check on her.

At the hospital, Tom gently held Marvin's hand and prayed, "Father, in the name of Jesus, I have a covenant with You. According to Hebrews 13:5, You said You would never leave me nor forsake me. I call forth healing for our son."

Enochos, Tom's demon, began to taunt him. "This is what you get for hiding your secret. This is your fault! You know you should have gone to the car as soon as you saw Carla and the kids."

Tom's walk with the Lord was strong, so when he heard negative thoughts, he attacked and questioned them. "Even if this is my fault, all things work together for the good of those who love God and are called according to His purpose. No weapon formed against me shall prosper."

"Be gone! You have no place here," Etan, Tom's angel, said to Enochos.

Enochos left in sorrow because his job was to provoke Tom into saying something that would cause him to curse himself. In doing so, Enochos could call a posse of other demons to wreak havoc in Tom's life.

Tom refused. His motto was, "Let the words of my mouth, and the meditation of my heart, be acceptable in thy sight, O Lord, my strength, and my redeemer." He had strong faith.

Marvin was enjoying his time in Heaven. He saw children he knew and family members he had never met before. While there, he had a visitation from Jesus.

"You're Jesus!" Marvin said.

"I am."

"My father talks about You all the time. He really loves You."

"When you go back, I want you to tell your father what you saw and give him this message."

"Okay, what do You want me to tell him?"

"Tell him it's not his fault."

"That's it?" asked Marvin curiously but excitedly. "Okay!"

"No, I have some more things you must share at the appointed time." Jesus walked and talked with Marvin for a while. "I must go back to the Throne. Enjoy your time here because you will be leaving soon," He said.

"Okay," said Marvin. "Will I be able to come back?"

"When you have finished your course, you will return," Jesus answered. "You must finish your course."

Four weeks passed and Marvin was still in a coma. His neck and spine were in a brace. The swelling from the spinal injury went down and the pressure on his skull had also reduced. The doctors wanted to be sure Marvin had recovered from the craniotomy before performing the spinal surgery. They needed to reattach his spinal cord to his skull. It was a risky procedure and could leave Marvin paralyzed from the neck down. Meanwhile, the hospital bills were beginning to add up, but Tom was just glad his son was alive. He and Carla took turns watching him and continued to pray while Grandmom took care of the kids.

Chapter 9
Schemes

It was close to two weeks before the hearing when Tom felt a nudging from the Holy Spirit to visit Paul. "Oh God, how can I go see Paul now, knowing that he knows it was my father who killed his father? You and I know that he would never deliberately hurt Marvin. And yet, here we are. What would I say to him? What might people think? How do I let him know that I am sorry? Even though my son lies here seemingly lifeless, whether Marvin should live or die, I trust You. God, I need Your wisdom and strength. And then there is Elaine. She doesn't deserve this. Nevertheless, God, not my will, but Your will be done."

Carla entered the room. She saw Tom with his head down. "Is everything okay?" she asked.

"It's fine," Tom responded.

"The kids are at Grandmom's house; dinner is in the microwave, and TJ and Jane's clothes are on their beds," Carla said.

"Okay, thank you. Hey, do you mind if I come a little later tomorrow?" Tom asked. "I need to make a stop before I come back to the hospital."

"Sure," answered Carla. "Anytime I get to spend more time with Marvin is a blessing."

"Okay, I'll see you tomorrow." After he gave a gentle kiss to Marvin and one to Carla, Tom left the hospital to pick up his children.

Meanwhile, Chief Gore called a meeting. A loud whistle blew at a frequency that only demons or angels could hear. He summoned Lofty and Enochos. "Alright, you blundering idiots! Why isn't Paul dead? And why hasn't Tom killed himself? This was supposed to be a two-for-one kill."

Lofty, speaking with much fear and trembling, said, "They both have the Word of God in them, and their angels surround them day and night. Our plan is working," Lofty added hesitantly. "It's just going a little slowly."

"What do you have to say for yourself, Enochos?"

"Chief Gore, Tom is on the brink of a nervous breakdown, and tomorrow, he will be the icing on the cake for this 'two-for-one kill,'" Enochos said haughtily. "Tom is going to see Paul. I'll have plenty of time to guilt-trip Tom to death."

"I will have plenty of time to anger and mystify Paul. The jobs will be accomplished," Lofty reported happily.

Chief Gore looked at them with a serious expression and began thinking aloud. "Who is Elaine's demon?"

"Sane," said Lofty.

Chief Gore blew his irritating high-pitched whistle. Sane appeared. "You called, Chief Gore?" Sane said in a trembling voice as he bowed in fear.

"How in the world did Elaine make it through that surgery and back home? She is another person who should have been gone by now. All you dejected failures can't do anything right. Sane! Cause her harm so that Tom can't go to the jail tomorrow," hollered Chief Gore.

"But—" rebutted Sane.

"But what?" Chief Gore interrupted as he angrily hovered over Sane.

"Their angels interrupt our plans," Sane said cringingly.

Chief Gore blew another ear-piercing whistle that summoned a higher rank of demons more hideous and ruthless than Lofty, Enochos, or Sane. Nine of them appeared. This set of demons was called the Semainos, or "Meanies." They didn't talk; they just looked at each other and knew what to do. Semainos communicated at the speed of thought. They traveled in gangs and were relentless in their torment. They remind you of creepy shadows. They moved on people's emotions and agitated them in packs. Semainos were known to cause fights, crazes of fear, or just outright hysteria.

"Now, listen you rejects! Sane, you are going to haunt Elaine in her sleep until she gets so nervous and scared that she needs to go to the hospital. I want her blood pressure to be high. Enochos, you are going to guilt-trip Tom to the point where he does not want to go to jail to talk to Paul. Lofty, Paul better hang himself tonight! You have plenty to torment him about."

Chief Gore blew that ear-piercing whistle one final time, and all three demons disappeared. "Semainos, listen. You three are going with

Sane to ensure he does his job of tormenting Elaine. You are going to help make it worse. Go now; you know what to do!" Looking at the second group, he said, "You three Semainos are going to gang up on Pastor Tom to the point where he is oppressed. He will not be able to lift his head because of guilt and shame."

"You last three know what to do. Paul better not be alive in the morning!" Chief Gore sent the last three away. "Now, let's see how this plays out."

Paul lay in his jail cell, attempting to go to sleep. It hadn't come easy for him lately. Suddenly, thoughts of despair flooded his mind. It was Lofty and the first three Semainos. "You are a horrible person! If you killed that little boy, no one would forgive you, not even God! Loser! Murderer!" This went on and on. Paul put the pillow over his head, but it did not work.

He finally began to cry out to God, "Make it stop!" The bailiff went toward the cell and told Paul to be quiet. Paul cried out loud "I know I am guilty! Stop!" Aleichem wanted to help, but Paul needed to use the Word and Jesus' name. If he could just remember what he had learned.

Paul cried out, "God," with a loud voice. The bailiff told him to be quiet again. He kneeled by his bed and cried to God, "Father, You said You would never leave me nor forsake me."

As Paul prayed, Sandy, one of the church mothers, felt a quickening from the Holy Spirit. She was led to pray for Paul and began to intercede for him. "I bind up the spirit of suicide, depression, and guilt," she stated. "I command you to take your hands off Paul's mind right now in the name of Jesus!"

Lofty and the three of the Semainos screamed, "Who prays against us?"

"I plead the Blood of Jesus against the enemies of Paul's mind," Sandy responded.

A gut-wrenching scream came from Lofty and the Semainos. "The Blood! The Blood! We have no power against the Blood of Jesus!" they ferociously screamed. "Who prays against us?"

Aleichem reminded Paul of the Word of God. "Iniquities," Aleichem said.

Paul, still kneeling, replied, "God, I don't deserve Your mercy or grace, but Your Word says, 'You were wounded for my transgressions and bruised for my iniquities.' Your Word also says, 'There is therefore now no condemnation.' God, I don't know all the words to the verse, but I know that You love me. I call on You for my mind."

Aleichem blew his horn, and Lofty and the demons left. Paul got back in bed and finally went to sleep.

Meanwhile, Sane went to taunt Elaine in her sleep. As she began to drift off, she dreamed of something laughing and chasing her again. The entity would push her hard off a cliff. She tossed, turned, and talked in her sleep. Her blood pressure rose. The three Semainos entered the room and began to instill fear. She cried out in her sleep.

Mother Joan then felt a quickening in her spirit and began to pray.

Shamar, Elaine's angel, said, "Speak the Word."

Mother Joan woke up and began to pray aloud, "Thou shalt not be afraid of the terror by night, nor of the arrow that flieth by day. A thousand shall fall at thy side and ten thousand at thy right hand and nothing shall come nigh my dwelling."

Shamar said, "Weapon."

Elaine partially remembered and prayed, "No weapon formed against me shall prosper. I cast down imaginations and every high thing that exalts itself against the knowledge of Christ and bring into captivity every thought to the obedience of Christ."

Finally, Elaine and Joan, though not in the same room, said simultaneously, "The Blood of Jesus!" They were united by the Holy Spirit. Sane howled in bereavement. He could not cope with those words. The pack of demons began to screech and whimper like hurt puppies. Elaine unknowingly said to Sane in her sleep, "Be gone in the name of Jesus." Her blood pressure regulated, and she returned to a peaceful sleep.

Enochos was ready. He was going to guilt trip Tom to the point of no return. Tom lay asleep in his bed alone while Carla was at the hospital with Marvin. The kids and Grandmom were sleeping. It was Enochos' time. He said to the Semainos, "Come on. Let's get him!"

To Tom, he said, "You were the one that made your father angry the night he hit Paul's father's truck. Remember? Remember what you said? You said, 'You're not my father because you left my mother.' Then your father stormed out in anger. Now look, the man who actually lost his father hit your son. See how the tide has turned? Did you think you would escape? This is your fault!"

Tom was alone and exhausted. The Semainos stared at him and projected oppressive guilt toward him. He felt extremely bad but did not open his mouth; he just cried.

"There it is. You should do what any upstanding minister would do who caused two deaths—die!" Enochos said.

Etan watched, powerlessly, waiting for the Word of God.

Tom angrily retorted, "One person did die, but not two. Marvin shall live and not die and declare the works of the Lord! Blessed be the LORD my strength, which teacheth my hands to war, and my fingers to fight. There is, therefore, no condemnation to those who are in Christ Jesus, who walk not after the flesh, but after the Spirit. Greater is He that is in me than he that is in the world. I can't deny that I feel the guilt. I can't deny my past. I can't change what I did, but I know who holds my tomorrow! He who has begun a good work in me will perform it until the day of Jesus Christ. No weapon formed against me shall prosper! Every tongue that rises against me is condemned!"

Etan finally rose. He caused his size to grow exponentially to about 15 feet in the presence of Enochos and the Semainos. He let out a roar and blew his trumpet. There was a shaking in the spirit realm, causing the demons to scream in fear, pain, and desperation.

Enochos and the Semainos left, screeching. The lights in Tom's room flickered briefly. Tom looked around and said, "I really must see Paul tomorrow. I don't know what God is going to do." He turned out the lights and went to sleep.

Chapter 10
The Visits

The next morning, Paul woke up and asked to take a shower. He wondered about Marvin. *Is he okay? Is he alive?* Paul got dressed, went back to his cell, and lay on his bed for the rest of the morning. Around 2:00 p.m., the bailiff came over to tell him he had a visitor. Paul replied, "Great! It must be Mom again." Elaine had been visiting Paul at least twice a week since the hearing, and he was always glad to see her.

The bailiff said that it wasn't his mom. "It's Tom Rogers?"

Paul curiously sat up in amazement and fear. He wanted to see Pastor Tom but at the same time, he did not want to see Pastor Tom.

Paul walked to a conference area with multiple circular tables where inmates met their families and other visitors. As Paul glanced around the room, he saw Tom sitting at a table with his back facing him. Paul slowly walked over and looked at Pastor Tom, who turned and looked at Paul.

"What are you doing here?" Paul asked.

Pastor Tom looked at Paul with tears streaming down his face. "I wanted to talk to you." Both men were desperate to talk but did not want to cause a scene.

"I-I-I never meant to hit Marvin," Paul said distraughtly. "Is he okay? Is he alive? No one will tell me anything."

Pastor Tom looked at Paul with the kindest eyes. "I know you didn't mean it. I know you would never intentionally hurt my son. He's still in critical condition, but I believe he will be okay, and God has him. He had a craniotomy, and he's still in a coma."

Paul looked down at the floor. Pastor Tom reached over and put his hand on Paul's shoulder. "That's not the reason I came."

"I know," Paul looked up and said.

Pastor Tom nervously blurted out, "My father k—"

Pastor Tom tried to tell Paul about what his father had done, but Paul couldn't bear to hear it from his pastor. He cut Pastor Tom off and said, "I know. I know. I know."

"I blamed myself for many years for what happened," Pastor Tom explained.

"Why?" asked Paul. "You would have only been a boy when it happened."

"My father and I got into an argument that night, and he stormed off afterward. I thought that if he hadn't been angry with me, he wouldn't have left abruptly, and this wouldn't have happened."

"My father drank a lot after he lost his job," Paul explained. "Who could possibly know? All the what-ifs," Paul sighed. "He was drunk that night. It's no one's fault. But...why didn't you tell me before?"

"At first, I didn't know. But when I did find out, I didn't know how to say it. How do you say my father k—?"

Paul cut Pastor Tom off again and changed the subject.

"My lawyer is trying to make it seem like it was your fault that this happened. I don't want to do this. I'm facing 15 years to life in prison, and if I'm in jail, no one will be there to take care of my mother. I drank the night before the accident, but I wasn't drunk. I just didn't see Marvin."

"I've asked my wife over and over not to leave the children unattended in the car," Tom said. "My lawyer claims that you were drunk and speeding."

Paul looked down and didn't reply. "I am worried about my mom. She needs my help."

"People from the church have been reaching out to her. I just want my son to recover," said Pastor Tom.

"So do I."

"I don't blame you," Pastor Tom said, though grieving.

"And I don't blame you," Paul responded quietly.

"Time!" the bailiff called.

Paul got up from the table and walked away. Pastor Tom sat for a moment, then left to be with Marvin.

"God, when will this end?" Tom asked as he walked to his car. He arrived at the hospital to relieve Carla.

"How are you, Honey?" Carla asked.

"I should be asking you the same thing. You've been here all night."

"I'm fine," Carla said.

As Tom went to hug Carla, he noticed that Marvin's eyes were fluttering more and his mouth moved as if he were talking. Marvin seemed to be carrying on a conversation with someone in his coma.

"Look!" Tom excitedly exclaimed to Carla.

"Oh, God!" Carla said gratefully. "Help! He is talking! He's talking!" she called out to the doctors and nurses.

Marvin was functioning in two worlds at this point. His spirit was still responding to his visit to Heaven, where he was playing with friends and talking to people there. Dr. Good came in and examined Marvin. "It's a good sign that he is talking. I still need to check and see if the swelling has gone down. I will contact the neurologist. This is good news!"

"God is moving," Tom said to himself. "Marvin is going to be okay; I just know it."

Marvin was not aware that his spirit was in Heaven but was responding on Earth. While his parents heard bits and pieces of the conversation he was having, Marvin's angel appeared to him.

"Hey, I was just playing with Sal," Marvin said.

"You'll be going back soon," the angel said.

"Why?"

"You have an assignment to complete."

"Right, Jesus already said that. I can come back when my assignment is done. I just really like it here," Marvin said with a sigh.

"When you go back, your body will be different and in some pain."

"Why?"

"You were hit by a car. You won't be able to walk for a while."

"Okay, but I will walk again, right?" Marvin asked, concerned.

"Yes. It will be a testimony," the angel replied. "Don't forget to tell your father what Jesus said. Tell him what you saw and about the people you met. He will want to know. Tell him to write it down. Share with people what you have seen and heard."

Marvin began to slowly wake from his coma. Both his parents sat in anticipation of this moment.

"Carla, let's sing his favorite song, 'I'll Praise Your Name.'"

Marvin woke up. He looked at his parents and whispered, "Mom? Dad?"

Tom and Carla looked over at Marvin, knelt by the bedside, and Carla began to cry. She got up and went into the hallway. While she was out, Marvin said to his father, "It's not your fault."

Tom looked up and said, "Huh?"

"Jesus told me to tell you it's not your fault."

Tom was bewildered, excited, and relieved.

"Jesus said…" Tom repeated.

Dr. Good came into the room with a few nurses and said, "I need you to wait outside while I conduct an examination. Nurse Lisa, please get some water for Marvin. Nurse Chad, start taking his vitals."

Dr. Good examined Marvin and called for the on-call neurologist. They both conducted thorough examinations. When the doctors were finished, they came out of the room to talk to Tom and Carla. "He's alert, coming around, and hungry. These are all good signs. He's still going to need the re-attachment surgery after more of the swelling goes down," said Dr. Good.

"Can we see him? Can we talk to him?" asked Tom.

"Yes, of course. He keeps saying he has to tell you something and to get a pen," Dr. Good informed them.

Tom and Carla rushed into the room.

"I saw Jesus! The angel and Jesus told me to tell you what I saw."

"Carla, go get a pen and paper!" Tom instructed.

Carla ran to get a pen and paper and quickly returned.

"Start from the beginning and talk slowly," Tom said to Marvin.

He began to write down everything Marvin said in detail.

Marvin talked about relatives he had seen on his mother's and father's sides whom he had never met. He spoke about the scents and fragrances of God's presence. He mentioned the flowers and how they moved in response to a person's feelings. He spoke of the trees from which people ate. He said that people go to Heaven and all they want to do is reach the Throne and see God. He said that people dressed nicely, wearing white robes and various types of clothes.

"I got to play with the children. There were so many of them there, waiting to see their mothers and fathers. The angel said that these children were taken from Earth early. Everything was so much nicer than here. The colors were brighter, and the streets looked like they were made of white gold."

Marvin suddenly stopped, and his face changed. He then asked, "Why didn't you tell me that I had another brother?"

Bewildered, Carla began to cry, while Tom looked on in amazement.

"He was born after T.J. but didn't make it," said Tom.

"He was really nice and looked a lot like Dad," Marvin replied. "He had black, wavy hair and liked singing. Heaven is a lot like Earth. There are mountains, rivers, beaches, houses, and all kinds of people from different lands. The angels answer you before you even ask your question. It's as if they can read your thoughts. The Throne is amazing. Everyone goes there to worship God. There are thunders, flashes of lightning, shouts of praise, songs that the angels sing, and people bow before the Throne. His presence was so strong that I became overwhelmed when I went. The angel took me to a brook to get water and a piece of fruit so I could be strong. Dad, did you know that Paul's dad died?"

Tom almost choked again, "Yes, Son."

"I saw him. He told me to tell Paul that he loved him and couldn't wait to see him and his mom."

Tom just kept writing. He did not want to miss anything Marvin said, so he did not interrupt. He let him continue to talk. When Tom thought Marvin was done, he asked, "What is Jesus like?"

Marvin pondered and gave his father a strange look. "Jesus is love!" Marvin exclaimed. "I thought you knew this already. You talk about Him and His presence all the time."

"I have been in the presence of the Holy Spirit, but I don't think I have met and seen Jesus in person like you have."

"Dad, I don't know how to say this, but you have seen Jesus daily. When you talk with Him, He is there. When you sing to Him, He is there. When you tell others about Him, He is there. We are guided by the Holy Spirit, and we have a lot of angels that help us. I know because I saw them when I was leaving to go to Heaven. I saw your angel, Mom's angel, and my angel. Do you remember when you taught me that big word?" Marvin asked. "Omni—"

"Omnipresent," confirmed Pastor Tom.

"Jesus is in Heaven, and I saw Him, but because the Father, Jesus, and the Holy Spirit are one and connected, they are still everywhere. I mean, think about it like this: God can answer your prayers and other people's prayers around the world at the same time."

Pastor Tom knew that his son meant well and was not lying. It was just that he had learned something different in seminary. He decided to change the subject. "Well, Son, I'm sure glad that you are here! I missed you all this time."

"What do you mean?"

Tom's cell phone rang. "Hey, Buddy, I got to take this. I'll be right back."

Tom walked out to take the call. When he was done, the nurse walked by and asked, "Are you okay?"

"Yes, why?" Tom replied.

"Well, I heard that your son says he went to Heaven. Children say the darndest things. Do you think that he actually—"

"Ma'am, I don't think. I know my son is telling the truth," Tom said, interrupting the nurse.

The nurse fell silent, and Tom returned to the room. Carla was holding Marvin's hand. Marvin was not placed in a typical bed after the accident; he was positioned upright with an apparatus that held his back semi-tilted toward the wall. He had a helmet on his head and was strapped in a position so that he could not move. Nurses came in to bathe Marvin, change his IV, and massage his legs for circulation. Now that he was awake, he wanted real food and to be let loose. The doctor said he could start with Jell-O and soft foods.

"Hey, Bud, I am so glad you're here. Your mom and I will be here tonight, and then I have to go in the morning."

Marvin was glad to see his parents. "Dad, I have some more I want to tell you about. Did you know we asked to come here?"

Chapter 11
The Trial – Part One

A week passed. It was three days before the trial. Out of concern, Reese went to visit Paul. "You have a visitor," the bailiff said. "Reese Canalti." Paul got up, and the bailiff escorted him to the conference room. Reese was sitting at the table. Paul was happy to see her.

"Hi, Paul!" Reese said excitedly.

Paul grabbed Reese's hand.

"No touching," the bailiff said.

Paul pulled his hand back.

"I miss you. I have been checking on your mom," Reese said.

"Thank you. I saw Pastor Tom."

"Wow! Is that allowed?" she asked.

"Oh, I don't know at this point, but I won't tell my lawyer. How's Ma?"

"She seems to be holding up. People from the church have been helping her. She said she should be able to go back to work soon. Paul, I am so worried about you," Reese said sadly. "What's going to happen?"

"My worst-case scenario is life in jail. My best-case scenario is not to go to jail and be on probation for five years. The in-between would be five to seven years with parole in about five years. I'm praying for the best-case scenario."

"I know you would never hurt anyone intentionally." Reese talked to Paul for a little while and then she left.

Back in his cell, Paul thought to himself, *what is going to happen if I get five years and parole? Where am I going to work? How am I going to support my mother? Where am I going to live? I probably already lost my apartment by now. What am I going to do? What church would I attend? No one wants to be bothered with me.* He prayed, "God, I don't know what to do, but I will be okay with whatever You decide."

The next day, Paul received another visit from his lawyer. He anxiously walked into the conference room and saw Mr. Levi who did not waste any time. "How are you, Paul? I want to go over the facts of the case. Your blood alcohol level at the time of the accident was 0.35. This is below the limit. So, while you may have been slightly hungover, you were not drunk. Mrs. Rogers was negligent in leaving three children in the car to go see her husband in the office. Witnesses say that Marvin did get out of the car and dart out in front of your car. As we speak, Marvin is alive talking and eating."

Tears welled up in Paul's eyes and his heart beat fiercely when he heard Marvin's name. "So, Marvin is going to be, okay? Right?" Paul asked.

"That's debatable," Mr. Levi stated. "Marvin may still need surgery. The plaintiffs have offered a plea bargain. If you plead guilty, they will give you three years in jail with no parole. After you serve your time, you just walk. If you continue with the trial, you're at the mercy of the judge and you know your options. You don't have to say anything now. You have until right before the trial to respond."

Mr. Levi said a few more words and then left. Paul went back to his cell and asked God what to do. He prayed, "God, I know I made a mistake. I would never hurt Marvin. I don't know what to do." He felt a certain peace and went to sleep.

Lofty thought this was the perfect time to disturb Paul and make him feel guilty. However, Aleichem quickly blocked him and said, "Not so! It is his divine visitation. Be gone." Lofty snarled and left Paul alone.

While Paul was sleeping, Aleichem took him to Heaven.

"Hey, don't I know you?" Paul said.

"My name is Aleichem."

"Where are we going?"

"You have an appointment."

Paul stood in shock as he traveled at what seemed like the speed of thought. He saw stars, galaxies, and supernovas, and then he arrived in Heaven. Upon his arrival, he saw a beautiful entrance with people in white robes. There were colors he had seen before and some he had never seen. The aroma of Heaven could not be replicated. You did not just smell it or ingest it; you felt it, breathed it, and it sweetly became a part of your existence. The most beautiful flowers or most comforting arousals from perfume could not embrace or compare to the holy breath of God. Aleichem took Paul through the gate. He saw people from the

Bible like Abraham, David, and Moses, as well as Mark and Luke. As Aleichem led him to his destination, Paul asked, "Please let me know where I am going."

Aleichem stopped. "This is the reason you are here."

Paul halted, and there was his father. Paul ran to him, hugged him, and cried. "How did you get here?" Paul asked curiously.

"I asked God to forgive me before I left the bar. I told myself and God that I was going to go home to your mother and make things right. I was tired of drinking and being miserable. I just did not make it home." Paul listened with relief.

His father went on, "Paul, Paul, there's a purpose in this struggle. You have a destiny to fulfill."

After hugging his father again, Paul asked, "What do you mean?"

"You are going to get out of prison. God is going to use you in this situation. Marvin will live and do great things for God because of this as well. Do not give up!"

"The people hate me," Paul said.

"The people are not your concern. Stay close to God; listen to Him, and obey," his father said.

Paul woke up from what felt like a dream. But he knew that it wasn't. He had this unexplainable peace.

The next morning, he got ready for the trial. He put on the suit that Attorney Levi bought for him to wear. Attorney Levi arrived at the court at 8:00 a.m. and requested that Paul arrive at 8:30 to go over the procedures. Once Paul arrived, he met Attorney Levi in a room. "Have you decided what you are going to do?" Mr. Levi asked.

"I want to go to trial. I will not take the plea bargain," Paul looked up and said.

"Very well. This is how the trial will go. Mr. Kategoros will go first with the opening statements. He intends to prove that you were driving under the influence and speeding and that you intended to hurt Marvin. Be careful how you answer him because he is shrewd. I will then give opening statements and afterward, Mr. Kategoros will bring his witnesses. Then I will cross-examine his witnesses, and at that point, I will be able to call our witnesses," Mr. Levi said.

Paul remained silent, even though he did not know who his witnesses were. He was at peace. He knew that he had heard from God through his father in his dream.

Paul and Attorney Levi entered the courtroom.

"All rise," ordered the bailiff.

Judge Gracen entered the courtroom.

"Please take your seats," said the bailiff.

"We are here for the case marked 'The State vs. Paul Gray,'" stated Judge Gracen. "Mr. Kategoros, please make your case."

"The State aims to prove that Mr. Gray was drinking the night before the accident. We also aim to prove that Mr. Gray was negligent and speeding, which caused Marvin to get hit by Mr. Gray's car. We also plan to prove that this incident was not an accident but a deliberate act of revenge by Mr. Gray. We are seeking the maximum penalty under the law."

Paul was angered by Mr. Kategoros' statement. He put his head down and let the tears roll for a minute. Attorney Levi gave him a tissue. "Keep it together," Mr. Levi said.

"Mr. Gray, do you understand the charges that have been brought against you?" Judge Gracen asked.

"I understand," Paul replied.

"How do you plead?"

"We plead not guilty," answered Attorney Levi.

The courtroom was again packed with people from the church and community. A small buzz filled the air.

"I understand that a plea bargain was offered," said Judge Gracen.

"Mr. Gray is rejecting the proposal. We aim to prove Mr. Gray's innocence. While he may have been drinking the night before, he was not legally drunk. We will also demonstrate that he was not seeking revenge; this was merely a tragic mishap due to unfortunate circumstances," said Attorney Levi.

"Okay, let's proceed," said Judge Gracen. "Mr. Kategoros, please present your opening statements."

Mr. Kategoros was witty and had a dramatic play with words. He painted Mr. Gray as if he were a sick monster. When he completed his daunting soliloquy, Judge Gracen stated, "Please call your first witness."

He began his argument. "Your Honor, Mr. Gray seems to have a history of drinking, much like his father. On the day of the accident, Mr. Gray admitted to the police that he had been drinking. He also admitted to hitting Marvin Rogers and did nothing to help the family when Marvin was struck by his car. He did not even get out of the car; instead, he just sat in his car and watched the family suffer. He willingly took the breathalyzer test and knew he was suffering from a hangover on his way to work. What is also interesting is that 15 years ago, Mr. Rogers' father was responsible for the death of Mr. Gray's father. The state does not believe that Marvin being hit was an accident but rather an act of revenge."

Mr. Kategoros' first witness was Cal. It pained him to be part of the process, but he had been subpoenaed. "Mr. Tomas, how do you know the defendant?"

"Please call me Cal."

"Okay, Cal," said Attorney Kategoros.

"He is one of the workers at the construction site," answered Cal.

"How long has he been at Ted's Construction?" asked Attorney Kategoros

"Oh, I don't know, over 20 years."

"Is he dependable?"

"Yes."

"Has he ever been late?"

"Yes."

"Could you describe his behaviors at the construction site when he has been late?"

"He usually rides kinda fast into the site and then rushes to the office to sign in," answered Cal.

"Is he frequently late?" asked Attorney Kategoros.

"He has not been lately except for the day of the incident."

"Please describe to the court what you saw the day of the incident."

"Paul was about three to five minutes late. He drove into the construction site as if he were in a rush. Mrs. Rogers had parked the car with the children in front of the office and went inside. When Paul was heading to his parking spot, Marvin ran out of the car. Paul hit Marvin with his truck; Marvin was thrown into the air and fell on his head," explained Cal.

"What did Paul do after that?"

"He sat in his car and did not move."

"Did he offer help?"

"No."

"So, your testimony is that after he hit Marvin, he did nothing."

"Yes," Cal solemnly stated.

Turning toward Judge Gracen, Attorney Kategoros said, "No further questions, Your Honor."

Judge Gracen looked at Mr. Levi and asked, "Do you have questions for this witness?"

"Yes, Your Honor."

"Proceed."

Attorney Levi proceeded, "You said that you saw Paul hit Marvin and then Marvin went into the air, fell, and hit his head. Is that correct?"

"Yes," replied Cal.

"Where were you standing when you observed the incident?"

"I was standing at the quarry."

"Your Honor, may I present Exhibit A?"

"You may," answered Judge Gracen.

"This is a map of the construction site. The quarry is about 50 feet from where the event occurred. Now, Mr. Cal, don't you wear glasses?"

"Yes, I do."

"Why?" asked Attorney Levi.

"Because I am near-sided."

"Please tell the court what that means."

"I don't see very well from far away without my glasses."

"About how far can you see clearly without your glasses?"

"I can see about 10 feet without my eyes going blurry."

"Were you wearing your glasses the day of the incident?"

There was a brief pause and silence. Cal grabbed his collar, and he took a deep swallow before answering. "No, I was wearing my goggles, not my glasses."

"So, if you can only see 10 feet without your glasses, how were you able to see the incident at 50 feet away?" questioned Mr. Levi.

"I heard that was what happened and when I ran over and saw the little boy bleeding out, I believed what I heard."

"So, you never saw the incident occur? You went based on what you heard?"

"Yes."

"No further questions for this witness, Your Honor."

"Mr. Kategoros, please call your next witness," Judge Gracen said.

"I call Carl Santiago to the witness stand."

Carl also did not want to testify but was subpoenaed. When Carl saw Paul, he was very distraught as he took the witness stand. He felt an enormous amount of guilt about the situation because he was the one who ordered all the drinks for Paul.

Carl was sworn in. "Do you swear to tell the truth, the whole truth, and nothing but the truth so help you God?" asked the bailiff.

"I do," answered Carl.

"Please proceed, Attorney Kategoros," said Judge Gracen.

"How do you know Mr. Paul Gray?" questioned Mr. Kategoros

"We used to meet at Charlie's Bar."

"Please tell the court what happened the night before the incident."

"It was a Thursday night. I asked Paul to come watch the game and have drinks with me. Paul came. He drank soda at first. I teased and harassed him a little bit about not drinking. I bought him a couple of rounds and he wouldn't drink at first. Later, when the game was getting good, Paul had about three drinks. He then drove off. I guess he went home."

"Do you think he was drunk?" Mr. Kategoros asked.

"Objection, Your Honor! Mr. Carl has no way of knowing this, Your Honor. He is not a toxicologist," exclaimed Attorney Levi.

"Sustained," Judge Gracen stated. "Do you have any further questions?"

"No, Your Honor," said Mr. Kategoros.

"Mr. Levi, do you want to cross-examine?"

"Yes, Your Honor. You said that you bought him a couple of rounds to drink. What did you buy him?" asked Attorney Levi.

"I bought him three beers on ice."

"So, by the time he consumed them, his drinks were watered down?"

"I guess," said Carl.

"Objection, Your Honor!" Mr. Kategoros shouted. "He can't prove that either."

"Sustained," said Judge Gracen.

"What caused you to want to buy Paul the alcohol?" Attorney Levi proceeded.

"Objection, Your Honor! That cause has no bearing on this case."

"Overruled. Proceed," said Judge Gracen.

"Mr. Carl, why were you trying to get Paul to drink?"

"Truth be told, I missed my friend. Paul started going to church and not coming to the bar anymore after his mother got sick. We used to hang out and drink all the time. It was selfish of me," said Carl. "I just wanted to relive old times. If I had known all this would have happened, I would've never done so."

"Your Honor, strike against the witness. He cannot prove that Paul's drinking was the reason for the incident," said Attorney Levi.

"Sustained," Judge Gracen stated. "Do you have any more questions for the witness?"

"No, Your Honor."

"Mr. Kategoros, do you have any more witnesses?"

"Your Honor, I would like to call Mrs. Rogers."

"Mrs. Rogers, please take the stand."

A small buzz of conversation transpired when Mrs. Rogers' name was called. She quietly went to the stand and looked back at Pastor Tom. The bailiff swore her in. "Do you swear to tell the truth, the whole truth, and nothing but the truth so help you God?"

She put her right hand on the Bible and said, "Yes."

"Mrs. Rogers, please tell the court what happened," Attorney Kategoros began.

"I woke up in the morning and got myself and the children ready for school. I forgot to give Tom the tickets for the church raffle, so I said I would drop them off to him before taking the kids to school. When I arrived, I got out of the car and went into the office to give Tom the tickets. All the children were in their seatbelts in the back of the car on their iPads. I thought everything was fine. I was only going to be a minute. When I went in to give Tom the tickets, I heard a horn blow and a screech. I came out and there was Marvin on the ground with his head bleeding. I ran to him. Mark called 9-1-1, and Paul just sat in his car. I cried and prayed."

Mrs. Rogers could barely keep her composure as she told the story.

"What did Mr. Rogers do?" asked Attorney Kategoros.

"He came out and started praying. We were afraid to touch Marvin because he was so badly hurt."

"What did Paul do?"

"He just sat there in shock, I guess."

"Did he say he was sorry?"

"No."

"Did he offer to do anything?"

"No."

"Did the ambulance and police come to the scene?"

"Yes, Tom rode in the ambulance with Marvin to the hospital. I drove the kids with me to the hospital. I called my mother to come meet us there."

"Did you say anything to Paul?"

"No."

"No further questions, Your Honor."

"Do you have any questions for this witness, Attorney Levi?" asked Judge Gracen.

"Yes, Your Honor. You said you went into the office to drop off the tickets. How long would you say you were in the office prior to the incident?"

"I think I was only there about 30 seconds."

"So, the children were left alone for about 30 seconds?" asked Attorney Levi.

"Yes..." Carla started crying. "I know what you're implying. You're saying I am not a good mother. I would never intentionally put my children in harm's way. I know what you're trying to say. You're saying it's my fault Marvin got hurt. If I hadn't left the children in the car alone, this wouldn't have happened."

"Objection, Your Honor! I move to strike the last part of the witness' testimony due to emotional distress," exclaimed Attorney Kategoros.

"Sustained," said Judge Gracen. "Mr. Levi, do you have any more questions for the witness?"

"Yes, just one more. Do you blame Paul for this accident?"

"As much as I wanted to know how Mr. Gray did not see Marvin, I cannot blame him," stated Mrs. Rogers. "I ponder in my head that even if I had called Tom out to get the tickets, would we be in this courtroom having this questioning because it was Tom who would have been hit instead of Marvin? It was just an accident," Carla said crying. "It was just an accident!"

"No further questions, Your Honor," said Attorney Levi.

"Mr. Kategoros, do you have any more witnesses?"

"No, Your Honor."

Carla left the witness stand in tears. Pastor Tom comforted her when she went to her seat.

"Mr. Levi, do you have any witnesses?" asked Judge Gracen.

"Your Honor, I'd like to call Ms. Reese Canalti."

Reese came to the stand and was sworn in.

"How do you know Paul?" asked Mr. Levi.

"We met about eight months ago. We go to the same church. We'd been seeing each other for about three months before the incident."

"What is Paul like?" asked Mr. Levi.

"He is kind, a little rough around the edges, and thoughtful. He likes to be by himself."

"Did he ever act as if he would ever intentionally hurt anyone?"

"No, Paul is not like that. He wouldn't intentionally hurt anyone."

"No further questions, Your Honor."

"Do you have questions for the witness, Mr. Kategoros?" asked Judge Gracen.

"Yes."

"You may proceed," said Judge Gracen.

"You said that you met Paul eight months ago. Is that true?"

"Yes," said Reese.

"You described him as kind, a little rough around the edges, and thoughtful. Is that true?"

"Yes."

"Please tell the court what you mean by a little rough around the edges."

"Sometimes, he can be a little sarcastic. Nothing worth worrying about," Reese said.

"Did you know that Paul drank?"

"Yes and no," Reese stated.

"What do you mean?" asked Attorney Kategoros.

"Well, I knew he stopped drinking when he started going to church."

"Did you know he was going to the bar to watch the game?" asked Mr. Kategoros.

"Yes," replied Reese.

"Did you know he was going to drink?" asked Attorney Kategoros.

"No, but I encouraged him not to."

"Why would you have to encourage him not to drink?"

"The Bible says corrupt companions corrupt good manners. Simply put, people who drink could influence you to drink."

"So, your testimony is that you have known Paul for eight months. Paul is sarcastic, hangs with corrupt people, and may drink. And you know that he would never hurt someone intentionally," said Mr. Kategoros.

"He is not perfect. No one is," said Reese. "I stand by my word that he would never hurt someone deliberately."

A small conversational buzz went through the room.

"Order in the court! Order in the court!" Judge Gracen demanded.

The people in the courtroom went silent.

"No further questions, Your Honor."

"You may go to your seat," said Judge Gracen.

Reese went to her seat and sat with Ms. Elaine who whispered to her, "It is okay." Reese was upset and Paul felt upset for her, but he said nothing. He just watched.

"We are going to take a brief recess," announced Judge Gracen. "We will reconvene in 20 minutes." Judge Gracen hit his gavel. People walked out of the room. Paul was taken to a meeting room within the court.

Chapter 12
The Trial – Part Two

Chief Gore attended the hearing and was quiet. Of course, no one could see him. As he watched the proceedings, he was frustrated and infuriated about how the lower demons failed their assignments, so he banished them.

If you want something done, you have to do it yourself, he said to himself. "I am going to make this judge hate Paul."

The judge went to his chambers to think. *Why didn't Paul see Marvin?* he asked himself.

Chief Gore entered the room. "You know why. He was drunk, and you know it," said Chief Gore. Although Judge Gracen could neither see nor feel Chief Gore, he could receive thoughts and images in his mind sent by Chief Gore. "No, I read the evidence. He was not legally drunk. So why didn't he see Marvin?" said Judge Gracen. "I hate drunk drivers with a passion. I will not tolerate it, but why does this case seem so different?"

The court was called to order. Everyone was seated. "Mr. Levi, please call your next witness."

"My next witness is Mr. Ezra, the toxicologist."

Mr. Ezra was sworn in.

"What were Mr. Gray's alcohol levels when you bought him in on the day of the incident?"

"The report states that Mr. Gray's alcohol level was 0.07."

"What is the OVI for the state of Ohio?"

"0.08," answered Mr. Ezra.

"Was Mr. Gray considered legally drunk?"

"No."

"Were there any other drugs in Mr. Gray's system?"

"No, just alcohol."

"Is it safe to say that Mr. Gray was not drunk at the time of the accident?"

"He was not drunk," answered Mr. Ezra.

"No further questions, Your Honor."

"Mr. Kategoros, do you have any questions for the witness?"

"Yes, Your Honor," replied Attorney Kategoros. "Did you say the toxicology report stated that Paul Gray's levels were .07?"

"Yes," replied Mr. Ezra.

"Even though Paul was not legally drunk, would he still be considered intoxicated?" Attorney Kategoros asked.

"Paul did not demonstrate any of the five signs that would indicate intoxication. His speech was coherent; he was not confused; his balance was steady; his coordination was appropriate, and his behavior was not offensive."

"No more questions, Your Honor," Attorney Kategoros angrily replied.

"You may step down, Mr. Ezra," Judge Gracen stated.

Mr. Ezra went to his seat.

"Mr. Levi, please call your next witness."

"I call to the stand Pastor Tom," said Attorney Levi.

Pastor Tom was sworn in.

"Could you please tell the court what happened?"

"I was on the phone with a client. I knew my wife was coming to give me the tickets. When I turned around, she was standing at the door and trying to get my attention. I motioned for her to put the tickets on the desk while I was still talking. When she went to put the tickets on the desk, I heard a horn blow, a screech, and one of the crew members yell, 'Oh no! Call 9-1-1!' I quickly ran out and there was Marvin's body, seemingly lifeless on the ground with blood coming from his head. I heard the foreman talking to the dispatcher. I prayed."

"Did Paul leave the scene?" Attorney Levi asked.

"No, he just sat in his car in shock."

"What was your relationship like with Paul at work before the accident?"

"We would speak and have short conversations from time to time."

"Are you Paul's pastor?"

"Yes. He attends the church I pastor, Open Arms."

"How would you describe your relationship at church?"

"It is a good relationship."

"Do you still feel it is a good relationship, even though Marvin is in the hospital right now?"

"The relationship is strained but not bad," Pastor Tom stated.

"No further questions, Your Honor," Attorney Levi informed.

"Do you have any questions for the witness, Attorney Kategoros?" asked Judge Gracen.

"Yes, Your Honor."

"Proceed," said Judge Gracen.

"How long have you known Paul?"

"I think I have known him for about 10 years."

"How long did you know that this man was the son of the man that was killed by your father?"

"I found out about a year ago."

"Did you ever tell him who you were?"

"No, I was going to tell Paul. I just didn't know how to say it."

"Did you think he already knew?"

"Objection, Your Honor," stated Attorney Levi. "There is no way to prove that before this point."

"Sustained," said Judge Gracen.

"Has Paul ever been snippy or rude to you or your family members?"

"No."

"How do you feel about this situation?"

"Well, I believe that all things work together for the good. I believe that there is an enemy that wants to hurt people. I hate all the variables in this situation. Paul is a member of my church and a co-worker. I consider him to be a friend. He would never intentionally hurt anyone, especially my family. I'm ashamed that I never told him about my father. I'm torn because my son is recovering from an accident that almost killed him, and it was caused by someone I consider a friend. I am also torn because I believe I was the reason my father got into an accident with Paul's father. My father and I argued that day, and he left the house angry. If I hadn't argued with him, he wouldn't have hurt Paul's father, and this is what I have rehearsed in my head for years."

"You said you considered Paul your friend. Is that correct? Doesn't your Bible say that a friend loves at all times?"

"Yes."

"Doesn't your Bible also say that Jesus said, 'I call you my friends because I tell you what I am going to do'?"

"Yes," said Tom.

"If Paul is such a friend, how come you withheld the information from him?" asked Attorney Kategoros.

"I already told you. I was looking for the right time," answered Tom.

"No further questions, Your Honor." Pastor Tom went to his seat.

"Attorney Levi, do you have another witness?"

"Yes. Your Honor, the next witness will be reporting via the telemonitor. The parents agreed to allow Marvin to testify in court for this case. We call Marvin Rogers to the stand." The courtroom buzzed with excitement again.

"Order in the court! Order in the court!" Judge Gracen struck his gavel several times, and the court got quiet. He asked to mute the monitor. "Now I want order, quiet, and no funny faces or tears when this child speaks. He is a 5-year-old, helpless, little boy who just suffered a traumatic brain injury and accident. If anyone has problems with this demand, leave right now. If there is one outburst, murmur, or complaint from any of you, I will turn off the monitor, remove all of you from my courtroom, and proceed without any of you. Do you understand?"

The people in the court nodded in compliance. A large television was positioned in the courtroom, and Marvin appeared on the screen. A nurse was present in the room with him. The court could see that Marvin was in his special stand-up bed and immobile. A hush fell over the room as they observed Marvin on the television screen. The bailiff unmuted the monitor.

"Hello, Marvin. Can you hear us?" Mr. Levi said.

"Yes," Marvin replied.

"Do you swear to tell the truth, the whole truth, and nothing but the truth, so help you God?" the bailiff asked Marvin.

"I am not allowed to swear, but I promise to tell the truth. My parents won't let me swear," Marvin responded.

"Is that a yes that you will tell the truth, Marvin?" asked the bailiff.

"Yes, I will tell the truth."

A few people in the courtroom looked down and chuckled silently at his response. "Hello, Marvin. How are you?" asked Mr. Levi.

"I am okay," said Marvin.

"Marvin, do you remember the accident?"

"I don't remember much about the accident, but I do remember much about Heaven." The courtroom buzzed again. Judge Gracen was upset.

"If I hear one more outburst from anyone else in this courtroom, you will all be escorted out and not permitted back in except for the parties involved. I want total silence."

The court went silent.

"Please tell us what you remember."

"Mom went to give Dad something at work. I wanted to ask Mom for her charger for my iPad. I unbuckled my seatbelt, got out of the car, and ran to ask Mom for her charger and that is all I remember. Next thing I know is I am looking at my mom crying at the hospital and the doctors are working on my body. I was not there. I went with the angel to Heaven."

"What do you mean you were looking at your mom crying, and the doctors were working on your body? Weren't you in a coma?"

"It's like I said. I saw my mom and dad as I was going to Heaven with the angel."

"Did you ever see Mr. Gray's car?"

"No, but I did meet his dad. He was a nice man."

"Do you mean in Heaven?"

"Yes."

"No further questions, Your Honor."

Mr. Levi turned red. He felt he had made a mistake by asking Marvin to testify.

"Mr. Kategoros, do you have questions for this witness?"

"Yes. Hello, Marvin," said Mr. Kategoros.

"Hello," said Marvin.

"You said you unbuckled the seat belt and ran to ask your mother about the charger. Is that correct? Did you hear any cars?"

"Not really, I was just worried about my charger."

"How do you feel, Marvin?"

"My body is very itchy in this cast, and I can't move. I don't like that people have to take care of me, and I wish I could run and walk."

The audience just stared in awe with light whispers. They were fearful that they would be put out during Marvin's testimony.

"What do you know about Mr. Gray?"

"Objection, Your Honor! This bears no relevance to the case," said Mr. Levi.

"Marvin's answer is key to the question about intention, Your Honor," retorted Mr. Kategoros.

"Sustained. I will allow it," said Judge Gracen. "I will allow it. Marvin, please answer the question."

"I didn't know Mr. Gray much. I knew he worked at my dad's job because I saw him once and he went to our church. I knew his mom came to our church. But when I went to Heaven, I met Mr. Gray's dad. He told me to tell Mr. Gray that he loved him; he was sorry, and that it would be okay. Jesus told me to tell my dad that the accident wasn't his fault."

The crowd proceeded to murmur when Judge Gracen hit the gavel one time.

"You see, in Heaven, there are many people with many stories. I met my brother—"

"What do you mean that Mr. Gray's father said it wasn't his fault?" Judge Gracen interrupted Marvin.

"Well, Your Honor, my dad and my dad's dad got into an argument the day Mr. Gray's father died. My dad thought that if he hadn't argued with his father, the accident would not have happened."

"Marvin, do you really believe that you saw Jesus?" asked Judge Gracen.

"Yes, Jesus told me to tell you that you must let go of your anger for the man who killed your mother. Jesus said that if you want to see your mother again, you have to forgive."

Judge Gracen's face turned red. He struggled to keep his composure. "How do you know about my mother?"

"I don't, but Jesus knows everything. He said that you lost her when you were young, on your 10th birthday, and you didn't like the people who raised you."

Puzzled, Judge Gracen asked, "How do you know about my family?"

"I don't. Jesus knows everything. I saw a lady who had long red hair though. She told me to tell you to look in the family house under your mom's bed. She said she always keeps her promises."

Judge Gracen was intimidated by Marvin and wanted to save face. He turned to Mr. Kategoros and said hastily, "Do you have any more questions for Marvin?"

"No, Your Honor."

"We are going to take a one-hour recess and then reconvene."

"All rise," said the bailiff.

The court turned off the monitor, and Marvin was fed lunch. Judge Gracen left the courtroom immediately. He drove to the family house about 20 minutes from the courthouse. When he arrived, he unlocked the door and entered his mother's room. He had not been in the room for 20 years. He went over to his mother's bed and searched under it. He found a box with his name on it. He quickly took it from underneath the bed and opened it. There was a card that said, "From Mom." Inside was the train set he had wanted for his birthday that year. Beneath the box was a Bible, and in the Bible was a card. It read: *"Today is your 10th birthday. I love you so much, Son. I knew you wanted this train. I hope you like it. I also gave you this Bible so that you would learn God's Word. It is the only thing that will keep you. Please remember what I said. Forgive others so that Your heavenly Father will forgive you. I love you. I love you. I love you forever."*

Judge Gracen cried so hard. He took the box, went downstairs, locked the front door, and got into his car. *This has to be God*, he thought, before proceeding back to the courthouse. On his way, Chief Gore grew angry. He did not know Marvin was going to testify. In fact, he thought Pastor Tom, Elaine, and Paul would have been gone by now.

Disappointed that the demons had failed and that those saints were still alive, Chief Gore decided to take matters into his own hands.

After the recess, court was in session, and everyone was seated. "All rise," ordered the bailiff. It was Attorney Kategoros' turn to continue questioning Marvin.

"Your Honor, clearly, Marvin has suffered some very traumatic injuries, and the State believes his testimony may be compromised due to his current condition. Do you still want the State to proceed?"

"Please continue," said Judge Gracen.

Attorney Kategoros did not want to question Marvin. He seemed a little afraid and unsure of what Marvin might say.

"Hello," said Attorney Kategoros.

"Hello," said Marvin.

"Marvin, do you know the difference between when someone is alive or dead?"

Marvin was quiet for a few seconds.

"Objection! What is the relevance of this questioning?" Attorney Levi yelled.

"Yes, Attorney Kategoros. What is the purpose of this?" asked Judge Gracen.

This was Chief Gore's chance to use Attorney Kategoros to cause massive condemnation of Paul. "Your Honor, the court needs to understand the severity of how much Mr. Gray has hurt Marvin. The

State is seeking the maximum punishment the court will allow against Paul. The court should know why the State is making this claim against Mr. Gray."

"Overruled," stated Judge Gracen. "Marvin, please answer the question."

"So, yes and no. I know that the body can stay on the earth, but a person can still be alive. I am not sure," said Marvin.

"Do you believe that you went to Heaven?" asked Attorney Kategoros.

"I know I went to Heaven."

"What did you see?" Mr. Kategoros, influenced by Chief Gore, aimed to make Marvin look foolish.

"I saw people, trees, angels, big buildings, Jesus—"

"Your Honor, as you can see, Marvin has been so traumatized that he believes he has seen things that clearly do not exist."

Marvin was upset. "That's not true! I saw your son," Marvin blurted.

"That's preposterous! I don't have a son."

"Yes, you do," said Marvin.

Chief Gore tried to influence Attorney Kategoros.

"Tell him to look at how severely this boy has been traumatized," said Chief Gore.

"You see, Your Honor, this child is beginning to make up things."

Marvin raised his voice and said, "His name is John! He left Earth when he was two from being sick." Mr. Kategoros could no longer deny Marvin's statements. He stopped in his tracks, looked at the screen, put his head down, and silence echoed through the room.

Tom got up and said to Judge Gracen, "This is enough. My son does not deserve this. Please make Attorney Kategoros stop. It doesn't matter if anyone believes my son. I do, even if I can't explain it. No one asked me if I wanted to do this. No one asked me if I wanted to press charges. No one asked me if I wanted to testify. Your Honor, I ask you to please stop. This is a really bad situation. Truth be told, I don't know how we are going to get through this."

Tom turned slightly to Paul and yelled, "Paul, we don't blame you! It was a mistake! Judge Gracen, please stop this. I need to tend to my son. He's upset because he believes he did what God told him to do, and this attorney is trying to discredit him. I must defend him."

Mr. Kategoros had tears in his eyes. "Your Honor, the State rests."

Up until this point, Judge Gracen would have been banging his gavel until there was a hole in the bench. He couldn't. He knew that Marvin was telling the truth. "Attorney Levi and Attorney Kategoros, meet me at the bench immediately," said Judge Gracen. "This debacle has to end. I am ending these proceedings for now. After this, you two meet me in my chambers." The attorneys went to their desks. "The court will adjourn for the rest of the day. Court will reconvene for proceedings tomorrow at noon."

Chief Gore's plans were not working. Suddenly, Chief Gore heard an ear-wrenching siren. It was the Thanotoshi. He was summoned to their Council. In a moment's time, Chief Gore was before the wicked and staunch 11 council members. They were sitting on a bench. Chief Gore stood alone in the middle of their courtroom. "We see that there has been much press from those humans regarding that child of God called Marvin," stated one of the council members. "Your imbecile demons were failures. You even went to the courtroom yourself today and were not successful. What are you going to do?"

The Counsel screamed and hovered over the bench at him. Chief Gore stood in fear, almost trembling. "I—I—I know what I must do."

"Then do it or face the consequences."

Chief Gore was whisked away. He knew there had to be another tragedy or something he could do so that he would not get banished.

Judge Gracen met with Attorney Levi and Attorney Kategoros.

"Attorney Kategoros, you already know that some of your petitions are not going to hold up in court. Paul was drinking the night before, but he was not legally drunk according to the toxicology report. Attorney Levi, Paul did hit this boy, and he sustained extensive trauma," said Judge Gracen. "This part cannot go unnoticed. Attorney Kategoros, your allegation about Paul intentionally hitting Marvin will not hold in court because, as far as we know right now, Paul did not know that Pastor

Tom's father was the person who killed his father until after this accident."

"Someone has to pay for hurting this child," Attorney Kategoros anxiously replied.

"Did Paul have auto insurance?" asked Judge Gracen.

"Yes," replied Attorney Levi. "Our office is handling the bills, and the rest will have to come from a combination of private pay from Paul, Pastor Tom's medical plan, and state assistance because the child has been deemed temporarily disabled. My office is handling it," Attorney Levi restated.

"How can Paul afford you?" asked Judge Gracen.

"He can't. I do one pro bono case a year, and this one is it. Your Honor, Paul going to jail for an accident is not going to make this situation better," said Attorney Levi. "He will not be able to pay the bills he owes to the Rogers, help his mother, or repay his debt to society while locked up. This was an unfortunate accident. It is not vehicular manslaughter, criminal negligence, or even drunk driving. The child darted out of the car, and Paul did not stop in time. That is it! Does the State even have a right to charge Paul Gray? The Rogers did not charge him!"

Attorney Kategoros sat down, still thinking about how Marvin had called him out about his son. "How did he know? Did you tell him?"

"What are you talking about?" Attorney Levi asked.

"You've been telling that little boy to say those things. You have been coaxing him. Admit it!" accused Attorney Kategoros.

"Your Honor, no, I have not," replied Attorney Levi. "The truth be told, I haven't spoken to Marvin this whole time until the trial. I only spoke with my client. I subpoenaed the witnesses."

"The boy is supernaturally telling the truth," Judge Gracen solemnly replied. "No one could have known about my mother's present but a higher power. All the things he said have been verified," continued Judge Gracen. "Did you lose a son?" Judge Gracen cautiously asked.

"It was a long time ago before I came to this country from Greece," admitted Attorney Kategoros. "My previous wife divorced me after his death. No one here knew about it. I never told anyone except immigration when I became a citizen here in the States."

"Was his name John?" Judge Gracen asked softly.

"Yes."

Attorney Kategoros let out a cry. No one could console him. Attorney Levi stood quietly with his head down.

"According to the law, Paul has technically served his time. I may have no choice but to declare a mistrial because there is no evidence to support the State's allegations. You two are not to say anything to anyone regarding this conversation, or I will hold you in contempt of court. I will hear Paul's testimony and closing arguments tomorrow."

Chapter 13
The Closing

Chief Gore was happy there was such a gap in the trial time for tomorrow. With the time he had, he could start his plan. "Someone will have to suffer, and it will not be me," he said. "Who is the most vulnerable? It's not the Pastor and his family; they are heavily guarded by the church and their prayers. It's not Paul or Elaine; they are starting to get stronger in their walk with God. All these people and their Word, their Bibles, and their Holy Spirit," Chief Gore said jealously. He finally stopped and thought, "I know there's the one who keeps rejecting You! Carl!"

Chief Gore went to Carl's house. He was watching TV while his father was sleeping. Chief Gore began his rants toward Carl, "This is all your fault. You gave Paul those beers. You're a selfish, undeserving friend. Your father doesn't even know or love you. Everyone has left you. You have no friends. You should just—"

"Stop!" Carl yelled. He had no defense. He had an angel but no Word. He knew about God but had not given his heart to Jesus. "I will make this right," he said. "I will do the right thing tomorrow in court."

The Thanotoshi wanted souls. Chief Gore knew that if he could get one soul into the kingdom of darkness, maybe his position would be secure. If the mission is to steal, kill, and destroy, then this plan was working. Carl was either going to drink himself to death by tomorrow or go to the courthouse and do something to end his misery.

Suddenly, on the other side of town, Reese felt led to pray for Carl. She prayed for his safety, his well-being, and against the spirit of suicide and destruction. She prayed for some time and then went to sleep. Chief Gore was unaware of the prayer and was getting ready to cause more trouble for Carl.

Carl's father woke up in the middle of the night, looking for his long-departed wife again. He came into Carl's room with a cane and was about to hit Carl in his sleep, but Carl woke up and moved. His father yelled, "Where is my wife?"

"Stop!" Carl yelled while dodging blows from the cane. He tried to take the cane from his father, but he fought him for a while. Finally, after a short tussle, he stopped and began to cry. Carl was used to his father's episodes, but tonight was harder for him because of how Chief Gore taunted him earlier.

Carl called the paramedics so that his father could get checked out. As his father sat on Carl's bed, he looked at Carl and said, "Carl, there's my boy." He spoke to Carl as if he had not just tried to beat him a few minutes prior. "I love you, but you have got to move on. I am going to lose it soon and there will be no saving me at that point. I already made my peace with God a long time ago. Son, you have got to move on."

Carl cried. He only knew how to take care of his father and work. Even though his father was senile, Carl knew his father was right. His brothers had moved on; his mother was in Heaven, and his father needed more care than Carl was emotionally able to provide. The paramedics arrived and took his father to the hospital. Carl went with him to make sure he was settled and then returned home. He decided to call off work for the day. *What will I do? I have no friends and my family is gone. If I left this world, my father would go to a nursing home and my brothers would go back to their families. What do I have?*

The next day was the final day of the trial. The court was in session. "All rise," said the bailiff.

Judge Gracen entered the room. "Please take your seats," he said.

Carl made it his business to attend the trial.

"Attorney Levi, please call your next witness."

"I call Paul Gray to the stand." Paul had handcuffs on his hands and shackles on his feet, with a metal chain connecting them. He puttered to the stand and was sworn in. "Please tell the court what happened on the day of the accident."

"I woke up late after hanging out the previous night at Charlie's Bar. I rushed to get ready and drove to work. As I was driving and looking for a parking spot, Marvin ran out in front of the car, and I hit him. His body was thrown a few feet, and he landed on his head."

"What did you do?"

"Nothing. I was in shock and petrified. Everyone else was doing everything, and all I could do was stare. I had never hit anyone before, let alone a child. A strong sensation of guilt overwhelmed me. I talked to the police, and then I ended up in jail."

"Prior to the accident, were you aware that Pastor Tom's father was responsible for your father's death?"

"I did not know," answered Paul. "When the reporter asked me about this, it shocked me. The reporter deliberately accused me of trying to harm Marvin to get back at Pastor Tom. There could be nothing further from the truth. Pastor Tom reintroduced me to Christ, helped take care of my mother, and to my knowledge, is still trying to help her and take care of his family. He helped me get extra hours to pay my mom's house bills. He did everything except tell me about his father."

"No further questions, Your Honor."

"Attorney Kategoros, do you have any questions for the defendant?"

Just as Attorney Kategoros was about to answer, Carl stood up. He had entered the courthouse with small razors. "This was all my fault! I never meant to cause you any harm, Paul! It is time for me to move on!" he yelled. Carl had moved from his seat and was in the side aisle. Judge Gracen summoned the bailiff. When the bailiff approached Carl, he yelled, "Stay away from me!" and slit his left wrist. The people in the courtroom stepped away from Carl.

The bailiff slowly moved toward him and said, "Now, let's talk about this, sir."

"Stay away or I will go for my neck!" Carl replied.

"Carl, please stop! It was never your fault! It was an accident!" Paul shouted.

"You don't understand, Paul. I just put my father in the hospital again, and now I have nothing."

"Carl, you have me, and you have God. If you just let Him in."

"What would God want with me?"

"He loves you! I love you, Carl. You are my friend. If you do this, you might not see me, and you might not see your mother again. The road you are choosing is lonely. Please consider what I am saying," Paul pleaded. "Please try; please don't do this. No one wants this for you."

Chief Gore stood in the courtroom. He kept looking at him, subliminally projecting despair toward Carl.

"Say this with me, Carl, please. Father, forgive me. I am a sinner. I believe You died for me. I believe You care for me. I want You to come into my life and save me. I confess that You are Lord and make You Lord over my life," Paul pleaded.

Desperate for relief, desperate for hope, Carl repeated the words after Paul. He sat against the wall, bleeding and crying. His gut-wrenching sobs of despair were felt by all in attendance. An ambulance came to take Carl to the hospital, and the bailiffs took the razors. Immediately, Chief Gore heard the sirens and was pulled into a tormented place in hell. He screamed and hollered, but there was no reprieve for him.

The court reconvened, but everyone except the plaintiff and the defendant were asked to leave for the verdict. Judge Gracen had heard enough for the day. "Due to the overwhelming lack of evidence in this trial, I am declaring a mistrial. Paul Gray, you are free to go."

Paul was happy and relieved to be released from jail. Reporters hounded him for a few months. He lost his apartment and went to live with his mother. Paul found a job at another construction site because he could not bear to return to Ted's Construction. He also visited Marvin often and made sure to pay the bills that insurance did not cover.

Reese and Paul eventually started dating again. Paul stayed friends with Pastor Tom, but he and Reese decided to attend another church. Elaine improved, and her full retirement came through so that she did not have to work anymore.

Carl placed his father in a nursing home. He began attending church and started losing weight. He also created a new business and initiated an outreach at church for families dealing with sick loved ones.

Marvin regained the ability to walk after his last surgery. He eventually went back to elementary school, and Paul made sure to speak to him at least twice a month. Pastor Tom decided to write a book based on what Marvin had told him about Heaven, and it went on to become a bestseller.

From the Author – Dr. D.M. Raphael

It is important to always note your surroundings in the natural and spiritual realms. Use the Word and prayer to fight your battles. Ask the Lord to **teach your hands to war, and your fingers to fight for ....** We wrestle not against flesh...

About the Author

Dr. D.M. Raphael is a multi-talented author, songwriter, teacher, pastor, entrepreneur, and devoted mother. With a passion for marrying spiritual truths with education, she is deeply committed to leading others to Christ. Born and raised in the Philadelphia metropolitan area as the eldest of six siblings, Dr. Raphael brings over 30 years of experience in education, where she embraces innovative and multifaceted approaches to inspire and mentor youth. Her mission is to not only teach but also to transform lives through faith, education, and a heart for service.